W9-BVR-057

THE BIG SHRINK

Also by Sarah Mlynowski, Lauren Myracle,
& Emily Jenkins:

UPSIDE ★ DOWN MAGIC

THE BIG SHRINK

by

Sarah
MLYNOWSKI,

Lauren
MYRACLE,

and

Emily
JENKINS

SCHOLASTIC PRESS/*New York*

For Rachel Feld, with jumbo dumpling-size thanks for her support of this series

Copyright © 2019 by Sarah Mlynowski, Lauren Myracle, and Emily Jenkins

All rights reserved. Published by Scholastic Press, an imprint of Scholastic Inc., *Publishers since 1920*. SCHOLASTIC, SCHOLASTIC PRESS, and associated logos are trademarks and/or registered trademarks of Scholastic Inc.

The publisher does not have any control over and does not assume any responsibility for author or third-party websites or their content.

No part of this publication may be reproduced, stored in a retrieval system, or transmitted in any form or by any means, electronic, mechanical, photocopying, recording, or otherwise, without written permission of the publisher. For information regarding permission, write to Scholastic Inc., Attention: Permissions Department, 557 Broadway, New York, NY 10012.

This book is a work of fiction. Names, characters, places, and incidents are either the product of the author's imagination or are used fictitiously, and any resemblance to actual persons, living or dead, business establishments, events, or locales is entirely coincidental.

Library of Congress Cataloging-in-Publication Data available

ISBN 978-1-338-22151-0

10 9 8 7 6 5 4 3 2 1   19 20 21 22 23

Printed in the U.S.A. 23
First edition, September 2019

Book design by Abby Dening

E linor Boxwood Horace loved her family. Obviously.

She loved her demanding father, who could turn things invisible.

She loved her bossy, sporty older brother, Hawthorn, who had fire magic.

And she loved her giggly older sister, Dalia, who could make animals do whatever she wanted.

What Nory Horace did *not* love was being home in Nutmeg with the three of them for Thanksgiving break.

Four days was so loooooong. Nory missed living in Dunwiddle with her aunt Margo, who served pizza for dinner several nights a week.

She missed her tiny bedroom with the stack of library books by the bed.

And she missed her friends from Dunwiddle Magic School, who were braver and more unusual than anybody here in Nutmeg.

Nory looked at her hard-boiled egg. It sat primly in one of Father's special egg cups. She didn't want to eat it, so she spun it around and around.

"Nory," Hawthorn whispered. "Don't fiddle." Father had stepped into the kitchen to get more jam for Ms. Cheddarlegs, who had come for Sunday brunch.

Nory groaned. Ms. Cheddarlegs worked with Nory's father at Sage Academy, the fanciest magic school in the country. Father was the headmaster. Ms. Cheddarlegs was head of the history department. She was the kind of person who always wore pantyhose.

Ms. Cheddarlegs cleared her throat and rapped her own egg cup with a tiny spoon. "Elinor," she said. "Sage Academy now makes all students study the history of dreary men who wrote dusty old books. Do you study dreary men and dusty old books at your school?"

Ms. Cheddarlegs didn't *actually* say "dreary men" or "dusty old books," but she might as well have. Everything she said was *so boring.* Plus, spending Sunday morning with an Important Educator made Nory feel dumb.

Last summer, Nory had flunked the Sage Academy admissions test. She flunked because her magic was upside down. Or "wonky," if you were being mean about it. Only students with strong and typical magic got to attend Sage Academy.

Hawthorn went to Sage. He was sixteen years old. He was an excellent Flare. There were five Fs of magic: Flares, Flyers, Fuzzies, Flickers, and Fluxers.

Like all Flares, Hawthorn was great in the

kitchen. He could cook eggs in his hands, for example. And roast marshmallows and peppers. But that was everyday Flare stuff. For the Thanksgiving feast, Hawthorn had cooked the turkey, the stuffing, and the green-bean casserole using magic instead of the oven. Father had wanted him to show off his skills for the invited guests.

Dalia went to Sage, too. She was thirteen years old and she was a Fuzzy. That meant she had animal magic. She'd shown off for Father's friends as well. Her rabbits had done a hopping dance to the tune of "The Lonely Goatherd."

Nory had *not* been asked to show her magic to Father's friends. She actually thought they really might like seeing her dritten. To become a dritten, Nory fluxed into a kitten, then added some dragon. She became a combination of the two creatures—a winged kitten with fangs and fire breath. It was massively cool. When it didn't go wrong.

See, Nory was a Fluxer. That meant she could

turn into animals. Only, unlike typical Fluxers, Nory often mixed those animals up together.

For example, she might flux into a mosquito, but add in kitten, and become a mitten. Or she'd flux into a dolphin, add porcupine, and become a porcuphin. Or maybe a puppy with squid legs. A squippy!

But mixed-up animals were not the kind of thing Father was proud of. Even though Nory was getting so good at them.

At Dunwiddle Magic School, the public school near where Nory's aunt Margo lived, Nory was one of eight fifth graders in a special Upside-Down Magic class. With Ms. Starr as her teacher, being upside down was fine by Nory. It was even fun. The students in the class were learning to make the most of their unusual abilities, even when the going was tough.

But being upside down around Father?

Not fun at all.

Now he returned to the dining room. "Here we

go," he said, presenting a pot of strawberry jam to Ms. Cheddarlegs. "Homemade by Hawthorn."

Nory sighed and pushed back her chair. "May I be excused, please?"

Dr. Horace nodded.

"Thank you for the delicious breakfast, Hawthorn," Nory said. "Have a lovely morning, Ms. Cheddarlegs."

She zoomed to the kitchen with her breakfast dishes.

Dalia followed Nory. The two of them wiped the counters and loaded the dishwasher. Dalia sighed as she scraped leftover granola into the compost bin. "I know you get Fruity Doodles for breakfast at Aunt Margo's," she said.

"All the time," said Nory, grinning.

"I wouldn't mind some Fruity Doodles. Father is always talking about protein and fiber."

Huh, Nory thought, looking at her sister. Did Dalia, like Nory, also think Father was a bit much sometimes?

Dalia's eyes lit up. "Ooh, I have something to show you. Come to my room."

Upstairs, Dalia dug a paper shopping bag out of her closet. She presented it to Nory. Inside was an egg-shaped toy. It was made from something softer than plastic, something spongy and squishy. It was pale green, dotted with orange polka dots. "Go on," said Dalia. "Squeeze it really hard. You're supposed to!"

Nory squeezed. And squeezed again.

The egg jiggled. The egg wiggled.

After ten or so seconds, it cracked into two even pieces with a loud farting sound.

"Wait," Dalia said, bouncing. "Look."

From inside the toy egg, a bitsy toy dragon emerged.

Not a real dragon.

Not a *live* dragon.

Just the most awesome toy dragon in the world. Nory had been studying dragons at school. This one looked like a Parsley Dragon: green with orange stripes.

The toy Parsley Dragon waddled around. It flapped its bitsy wings.

"They're called Dreggs," said Dalia. "Like a *Dragon Egg*. Get it? All the kids at Sage have them. Some are special. Some are more ordinary. A Parsley Dragon is a pretty good one."

Dalia explained that the toy dragons learned more and more tricks the more attention you gave them. "Just like real pets," she said. "For example, they have to sleep for ten hours a night."

"But that's boring," said Nory.

"No, because they sleep when you sleep. You tuck them back into their eggshells, and in the morning you squeeze the shell and they wake up. They re-hatch, which is cool because the hatching part is always funny."

Dalia showed Nory two more Dreggs, both of them currently in their eggs. One egg was blue and the other was a grayish beige. Dalia squeezed them both vigorously. The blue Dregg hatched first with a giant fart noise. Out popped a tiny Luminous Dragonette. It fluttered its lashes adorably.

"Aw!" said Nory.

"Hi," crooned Dalia. "Hi there, cutie!"

She tipped the dragon onto her bed, where it stood on first one leg and then the other. It made a tiny firbling noise, the special, flutelike sound of that kind of dragon. Then it stretched its wings and began to glow a beautiful lemon yellow.

"Cool, huh?" said Dalia. She snapped the empty halves of the eggshell together. She nodded at the tiny dragon. "Now, wait for it . . ."

The toy dragon cocked its head. It hopped toward Dalia. "Play with me?" it said in a cute voice. "Play with me!" It jumped up and down. "Play! With! Me!"

Nory ran her finger down the toy dragon's back. It firbled and cooed. "So cute."

"I know," Dalia said. "You have to play with them twice an hour if you want them to learn more and more tricks."

"If I had one, I'd play with it all the time," Nory said. She watched as Dalia's beige Dregg wiggled and cracked. *Pthhhhhb!* Out hatched a miniature Sludge Dragon.

It blinked. Dalia put it on her bed, and it blinked again.

"Why isn't it doing anything?" Nory asked.

Dalia reassembled the empty beige eggshell and put it in her pocket with the blue one. "Um. I've kind of been ignoring it."

"Dalia!" Nory scolded. She petted the Sludge's head and waited for it to do something.

It didn't. It just sat there, being beige. Then it lay down and dropped its chin onto its front paws.

"I like my other ones better," said Dalia. "But if I played with this one, it would start doing stuff. Anyway, aren't they awesome?"

"Yes. I want one!" cried Nory.

Dalia smiled. "You can get them at Brilliant Ned's. Maybe Aunt Margo will take you?"

"I'll ask," said Nory. "They're the best toys *ever*."

Aunt Margo was a Flyer, and a very skilled one. She ran a one-woman taxi service—meaning, she *was* the taxi. She flew her passengers wherever they wanted to go, within one hundred miles of Dunwiddle. When she came to pick up Nory after the holiday, she swooped down from the sky like a giant bird and skidded to a stop on the sidewalk.

Aunt Margo was Nory's mom's sister. Nory's mom had died when Nory was little. Aunt Margo had spent Thanksgiving with her boyfriend, Figs, and his family. Now, at last, she was here to take Nory back to Dunwiddle. Hooray!

Nory ran down the porch steps and zoomed across the lawn to give her aunt a tackle hug. "I have spending money from Father," she cried. "Can we go to Brilliant Ned's? Pretty please?"

Margo wrinkled her brow. "Perhaps. How come?"

"For Dreggs! They're dragon toys!"

"Sure, why not?" Aung Margo said with a laugh. "But first, let's go inside. I want to see Dalia, Hawthorn, and your father."

Father and Aunt Margo chatted for an hour. They talked about grown-up things like winter coats and scheduling and "How was your holiday?" "Fine, how was yours?" Father thanked Margo for looking after Nory. Margo said it was her favorite thing in the world to do.

It was weird for Nory to have her two worlds mix. Life with Margo was pizza and flying, watching tiger-ball on TV and sleeping late on weekends. Life with Father was manners and chores, nutritious foods and homework. But whatever. Sometimes Aunt Margo made her eat nutritious food, too.

Anyway, the grown-ups were done quickly enough, and soon Nory and Margo were flying across town to Brilliant Ned's in Nutmeg.

The Dreggs came in packs of one, two, or ten. Some of the packs were more expensive than others, and they had fancier Dreggs inside. Nory had just enough money for the cheapest bag of ten. Ten! She could give one to every kid in her class, including herself, and still have two left over.

In the crisp evening air, Nory linked one hand with

Aunt Margo's and clutched her bag of Dreggs with the other. Aunt Margo grabbed Nory's suitcase and launched them both into the air.

It was twilight when they reached the outskirts of Dunwiddle. Nory thought the rooftops below looked cozy and welcoming. The houses weren't grand, but they were friendly-looking, lit from within. There was Pepper's house, with her little brothers' toys all over the backyard. *Hi, Pepper's house!* And Elliott's house, with an ice sculpture melting on the grass in front of it. *Hi, Elliott's house!*

There was Dunwiddle Magic School, and suddenly, right below them, Aunt Margo's small clapboard house, with its tiny backyard. There were the plants, the toolshed, the picnic table. And in front, there was Aunt Margo's small yellow car in the driveway. *Ahhh. Home.*

They landed and went inside. Nory ran up to her room and spread the Dreggs out on her bed. She couldn't tell which eggs held which kinds of dragons, although she wondered if the color of the eggs might provide a clue. Would the pink one be a Blurper Dragon? Or would it be the purple one instead? Would the deep orange one with red spots be a Tangerine Dragon or a Flaming Nugget Dragon?

Do Right by Your Dregg! read the directions that came with each. They explained what Dalia already said: Play with them lots. Pet them, tickle them, pat them, carry them around. That way, they will learn new tricks. Also, make sure they get their sleep by closing them into their eggs at night.

Easy-peasy, thought Nory.

The only hard part would be deciding which Dreggs to keep and which to give to her friends.

2

On Monday before lunch, Marigold Ramos adjusted the volume on her hearing aids. They were small and tannish-pink so they blended in with Marigold's skin. Most kids noticed the aids eventually, but before that, they noticed Marigold's creative fashion sense. Or her original way of thinking. Or her clarinet playing. And what really set Marigold apart was her upside-down magic.

Marigold was in Nory's UDM class. That meant that like the other UDM kids, her talent wasn't one of the typical five Fs: Flare, Fuzzy, Fluxer, Flyer, or

Flicker. For example, Elliott Cohen was an Upside-Down Flare. Elliott froze things instead of lighting them on fire. Willa Ingeborg was an Upside-Down Flare, too, but made water instead of ice. She caused it to rain indoors.

Pepper Phan was an Upside-Down Fuzzy. She frightened animals instead of taming them.

Bax Kapoor was an Upside-Down Fluxer, same as Nory, only Nory turned into mixed-up animals while Bax usually turned into a rock or a swivel chair. Or, one time, a player piano.

Andres Padillo was an Upside-Down Flyer. He could swoop high in the sky, but he had trouble getting down. Most of the time, he floated on the ceiling.

And last but not least, Sebastian Boondoggle was an Upside-Down Flicker. Typical Flickers could turn things invisible. Sebastian could not. He could, however, see things that were invisible to other people, like sound waves. Sebastian wore goggles to block the worst of the visible sound waves so that they didn't drive him bonkers.

Marigold shrank things. That was her magic. It wasn't Upside-Down Fuzzy magic, or Upside-Down Flare magic, or upside-down any of the other Fs. It just was what it was. She shrank things—and not always on purpose. She had no idea how to make them big again.

When her very, *very* unusual magic had come in, her parents hadn't known what to do. How could she learn to use her magic at their local school? None of the teachers would know how to teach her, or *what* to teach her!

Then her parents saw a TV show about a new school program for kids with upside-down magic. Would Marigold want to go live with Granddad Lorenzo and Grandmom Flora in Dunwiddle, where the program was offered?

Marigold said yes. She knew there was no way she could study magic with typical students. What class would she even be in?

So Marigold moved in with her grandparents. Sure, she missed her mom and dad. And yeah, she'd shrunk her grandfather's mattress, and his car. That had all been quite embarrassing. But she'd gotten used to life in Dunwiddle. And she loved her UDM classmates.

Now that she'd adjusted her hearing aids—it was crazy loud in the school cafeteria—she got a tray of school lunch and went to sit at the table they always shared. It was the first day back after Thanksgiving break. Everyone was full of talk.

"Hey-hey," she said to her best friend, Willa. Willa was the one who made indoor rain. Marigold wasn't sure Willa should really be called an Upside-Down Flare, though. Honestly, raining had nothing to do with Flaring.

If Marigold were in charge of the world, she'd say that Willa had water magic. She had told that to Willa, and the two girls decided maybe Willa was a *Fluid*, not an Upside-Down Flare. And Marigold thought of herself as a *Fitter*. That is, someone who *fit* objects into new sizes. In her case, smaller sizes.

Willa, a pale girl with straight blond hair, made

room for Marigold on the bench. "Nory brought presents! For all of us! Look!"

Everyone was holding up . . . what were they? Eggs?

"You squeeze the shell, like this," said Sebastian. He had a rosy round face and wore a shirt with a collar and his goggles. He flexed his fingers around a small magenta egg.

The egg rolled back and forth on his palm, then cracked in half with a farting noise that made everyone laugh. Out wobbled a tiny magenta Blurper Dragon.

"Whoa," said Marigold. That was insanely cool, probably the coolest toy Marigold had ever seen.

The tiny Blurper Dragon lashed its tongue.

"You got a Blurper," Nory cried. "That's the dragon in my dritten!"

"Yup," Sebastian said. He grabbed the Blurper Dragon and closed it back into its eggshell. "I love re-hatching him. It never gets old."

All around the table, eggs jiggled, then farted

and hatched. Andres, who was wearing his brick-pack to keep him from floating up to the ceiling, showed Marigold his miniature green Arbor Dragon. It opened its mouth and squealed.

"I love you, little guy," Andres told his Dregg.

"Here," said Nory importantly. Her eyes did that sparky thing they often did. "For you, Marigold."

She dropped a turquoise egg into Marigold's hand. "Oh, thank you," Marigold cried. She squeezed the eggshell the way she'd seen the others doing, and it hatched into a bright blue Bubble Dragon.

"Well, *hellooo*!" Marigold cooed. "You are the cutest thing ever. Willa, look."

The itty-bitty Bubble Dragon lifted its tail and farted. Everyone fell apart laughing. Marigold named her Tootsie.

"Play with her and she'll learn more tricks," urged Nory.

"Yeah?" said Marigold. She got straight to work playing with Tootsie and patting her on the head. Oh, she was adorable.

Lunch zoomed by, and before Marigold knew it, she and the other UDM kids were filing back into Ms. Starr's classroom. Everyone rushed to show Ms. Starr their Dreggs.

"They're very cute," Ms. Starr said. "Did that pink one—did she just wag her tail? Oh, my!"

She was the kind of teacher who truly cared about the kids. She kept her temper, made lessons fun, and never made anyone feel bad if their upside-down magic got out of control. She took the time to look at everyone's Dregg and then clapped her hands. "Now put them away. In your desks. I have an announcement."

It took longer than usual, but finally, everyone quieted down. Ms. Starr smiled straight at Marigold, and Marigold felt her tummy flip over. Everyone in the class had been assigned tutors to help them with their unique magics, except for Marigold. Ms. Starr had hinted before break that she had a possible tutor for Marigold.

Marigold tried not to get her hopes up . . . but maybe today was the day?

"Yes," Ms. Starr said, answering Marigold's unasked question. "I just got confirmation from Dunwiddle University's Department of Magical Studies, and *you*, Marigold, officially have a tutor!"

Willa reached over from her desk and found Marigold's hand. She gave it a quick, happy squeeze.

"Her name is Layla Lapczynski," Ms. Starr said. "She's a graduate student, which means she's finished college and she's studying to be an expert. So she's not a teacher. But she has size-related magic, just like you. And she's been doing her graduate research on how it works."

Size-related magic? For real?

"Your first meeting is tomorrow," Ms. Starr finished. "Oh, Marigold, this is such wonderful news, isn't it?"

Marigold grinned. "It is."

3

The next morning, Nory met Elliott so they could walk to school together. "Do you have your Dregg?" she asked.

"Duh," Elliott said with a grin. He patted his pocket. "I played with Groggy after my homework, and again after dinner, and first thing this morning."

"Does he have any new tricks?"

"Yep. Groggy can now wiggle his backside, thump his tail, and hop three hops," said Elliott.

"Sweet," said Nory. "Glowie's learning new things, too. She's a Luminous Dragonette, and as of this morning, she can turn green. But she doesn't fir-ble yet."

"Have you hatched your two extra ones?"

Nory shook her head. "Not yet. I'm saving them."

As they approached the redbrick building, Nory's heart gave a happy skip. Standing in the cool November air were all her friends. Except for Andres, of course. He was flying on his leash, while his sister, Carmen, held the other end, chatting with her eighth-grade friends.

Everyone—even Andres, way up high—was play-ing with their Dreggs.

Elliott squeezed his eggshell. "Everyone, look," he said as his Dregg wobbled and cracked, then made an especially hilarious farting noise as Groggy emerged. Groggy was a tiny brown Grog Dragon with eyes like firebolts. He thumped his tiny tail. He hopped back and forth on Elliott's palm and snapped his teeth.

"Zwingo!" said Sebastian.

"You didn't tell me he bit!" cried Nory.

"Cool, right?" said Elliott.

Sebastian's Dregg hatched, and out popped a miniature Blurper Dragon.

"Nory, look," Sebastian exclaimed. "My Blurper is saying hi to you."

"Hi, Blurper!" said Nory. As Nory watched, Sebastian's Blurper waved at her. Wow!

Pepper's egg had hatched into a murky-brown Mud Dragon. "I'm calling her Mudpie," she said. "I love her so so so so much!" Since Pepper's magic terrified animals, she couldn't have real pets. "Last night, I put her shell on my pillow so she could sleep next to me, and guess what? She snores. You can hear it even through her eggshell."

"So funny," said Nory. She was happy for her friend.

"Hey, Zinnia," called Pepper. "Come see the Dreggs. Nory got them for us."

Zinnia was a Flare who was a friend of Pepper's. Zinnia was okay, Nory thought. But she was also semi-friends with Lacey Clench, who was basically Nory's archenemy.

Zinnia came over and admired Mudpie. "She is just the cutest. Can I hold her?"

"Sure," said Pepper. "You can even put her back in her egg and make her re-hatch. You're the best, Mudpie. Yes, you are."

Zinnia got to business, fitting Mudpie back into the shell. "Now what?"

"You squeeze it," Pepper said gleefully.

"But I just—"

"I know." Pepper caught Nory's eye and grinned. "Squeeze it, Zinnia. Trust me."

"Oka-a-y," Zinnia said, squeezing the Dregg tentatively. "Hey, Nory, where do you buy Dreggs? Like if I wanted to get one for myself?"

Nory hesitated. She did have two unhatched Dreggs left. Okay, fine.

She reached into her pocket and handed a yellow-and-green-striped egg to Zinnia.

"For me?" Zinnia asked, eyes wide.

"Sure."

"Wow. Thank you!"

Nory glowed. She quite liked being the one and only Nory, giver of Dreggs. She could spare one for Pepper's friend. All was well with the world.

4

ater that morning, Marigold waited anxiously in the library for her tutor, Layla Lapczynski. She repeated Ms. Lapczynski's full name over and over in her mind, the same way Ms. Starr pronounced it, to be sure she got it right. *Lap-zin-skee.*

Zwingo. Marigold was a ball of nerves.

"Big day, huh?" commented the librarian, Mr. Wang. He had lines around his eyes and wore a brown cardigan.

Marigold nodded. Her mouth was dry.

"You'll do great," Mr. Wang said. "Don't worry."

He fluxed into a koala and hopped onto a bookshelf to tidy the top row of books.

Ms. Lapczynski was supposed to be there at ten a.m. That's what Ms. Starr had said. But by ten fifteen, no one had shown up.

What was wrong?

At ten nineteen, a young woman wearing ripped jeans, heavy boots, and a large fake fur coat strolled into the library. She was daunting and edgy, with pale skin, dyed blue hair, and a slim silver hoop in her nose. She reminded Marigold of a faerie.

"Hi." She came to Marigold's table and propped her hands on the top of a chair. "I'm Layla. Are you Marigold?"

Marigold nodded.

Ms. Lapczynski put her backpack on the table but didn't sit down. With a lazy grin, she said, "Well, cool. Let's do this thing. You ready to roll?"

Marigold nodded again, but she wasn't sure how the process was supposed to work. Ms. Lapczynski didn't seem very grown-up. And why wasn't she sitting?

With zero warning, Ms. Lapczynski *expanded*, right in front of Marigold's eyes.

She grew and grew, like a balloon being filled with air, until her head gently touched the ceiling.

Each of Ms. Lapczynski's fingers were now as thick as Marigold's arm. Her clothes grew larger, too. Her face looked big and moony. She was a giant!

Koala-Mr. Wang watched in awe from the top of the bookshelf.

"Whoa," Marigold breathed.

Then, gracefully, Ms. Lapczynski shrank herself back down until she reached her original size. "There," she said, taking a seat. "What'd you think?"

"Amazing!" Marigold said. "Ms. Lapczynski, that was—"

"Layla," her tutor interrupted.

"Huh?"

"Omigosh, call me Layla. I'm only twenty-three. Your turn."

Marigold blinked. "Uh . . ."

"Big up," Layla said, shrugging out of her enormous coat.

Marigold blinked. "Uh . . ."

Layla propped her elbows on the table and rested her chin on her hands. "Come on. Make yourself bigger. Like I did."

"I can't," Marigold said.

Layla furrowed her brow. "Would you rather make something else bigger, like a pencil or a book?"

"I can't," Marigold said. "I only make things smaller." Her spirits sank. Wasn't Layla supposed to know what Marigold could and couldn't do?

"That's why I need your help," Marigold pressed on. "I can shrink things, but then they're stuck. I can't *un*-shrink them."

"Huh," Layla said. "Guess I didn't get that memo."

Layla looked around the library. Her eyes brightened, and she hopped up from the table. She returned with a stack of books from the *M* fiction shelves: the Whatever After series and the Flower Power series. Marigold had read them both.

"Shrink these," Layla told Marigold, and she said it with such an air of command that Marigold just . . . did.

Ploof-whistle-puff! The books shrank until they were the size of Marigold's pinkie nail.

"Ni-i-ice!" Layla said, holding out her palm for a high five.

Marigold slapped Layla's palm with her own.

Koala-Mr. Wang scrambled down from the high shelf where he was working, leapt onto the table, and started examining the books.

Pop! He was human Mr. Wang again, and he was *not* happy. He jumped back to the floor and shook his finger at Layla. "Now, listen. Marigold just told you she can't make things big again. And yet you let her shrink my books? What were you thinking? The library has a limited budget."

Layla was already on her feet, thrusting her arms into her coat and heading for the door. She threw a thumbs-up to Marigold. "Same time next week? I bet I can teach you how to big up. Maybe. If your magic works like I think it does, I'll get you sorted out. I like you, Marigold!"

"Okay," Marigold called.

"Come back!" called Mr. Wang. "Resize the books now, please. They're school property."

The door swung closed. Layla was gone.

What just happened? Marigold's head was spinning.

Wasn't tutoring supposed to be like teaching? Layla hadn't taught Marigold *any*thing, except that there was someone else in the world who could magically alter something's size.

Which, now that Marigold thought about it, was pretty huge.

And Layla was going to teach her to "big up." That would be even huger.

She scrambled out of her chair and grabbed her backpack. "Sorry, Mr. Wang. We'll fix your books next week!" she called as she ran to the door. "Me and Layla. My tutor. We'll big them back up for you, I promise."

5

After-school kittenball club had been awkward for Nory at first, because of her upside-down magic. All the other kittenballers were typical Fluxers. But now, three months after she'd joined, Nory could hold her kitten shape for more than fifteen minutes, and the other players had gotten comfortable with her.

During club, Nory and her Fluxer friends worked with Coach Vitomin on kittenball skills so they could join the team, the Dunwiddle Catnips, in seventh grade. Coach was also Nory's fluxing tutor. He was a bald, muscly man who could turn into nineteen different house cats. He had a whistle he was fond of blowing and he ate a lot of health food.

Before practice, Nory, Finn, Akari, and Paige usually spent some time hanging out on the field. They ate chocolate and goofed around. Today, Nory brought Glowie.

"Zamboozle," said Akari.

"Double zamboozle," said Paige.

"I saw one of those at my friend's house last week," said Finn. "It's called a Dregg, right?"

Nory let them stroke the Luminous Dragonette. And then she dug the last Dregg out of her pocket and squeezed its silver eggshell. She wasn't going to give this one away, but there was no reason not to show it off.

Paige turned into a kitten and sniffed the silver egg.

Pb-b-b-b-b! It hatched. Out popped a tiny slate-gray Slipper Dragon. It ran toward Kitten-Paige ferociously. Kitten-Paige leapt back, her fur standing on end and her tail straight in the air. "Ha! That scared me," she said, fluxing back into a girl. "They look a lot bigger when you're small."

The Slipper Dragon stomped its feet and howled. Nory scooped it up and stroked its tiny head. The dragon howled again. "Hello, little one. I'll name you Howler."

"Where do you get them?" asked Akari. "I just got my allowance."

"Brilliant Ned's has them."

"Sweet," said Paige. "There's a Brilliant Ned's on my way home. We should totally go."

Coach appeared at the far end of the field. "Time for carrot juice," he called, waving a large thermos. "I have seaweed snacks, too. We'll eat while I go over the skills we're working on today. Then we'll Flux and get moving. 'Kay, kittenballers?"

"Yessir, Coach!" they shouted. But they stayed where they were. Newborn Howler was yelling. And Glowie was turning green.

"KittenBALLERS!" barked Coach. "Now, not tomorrow!"

"I'm totally getting a Dregg after practice," said Akari.

"I'm coming with you," said Finn.

"Me too," Paige said. "The other Fluxers are going to go nuts."

On Thursday, Elliott and Nory got to school early. Breakfast was served in the school cafeteria. Anyone who wanted could come and get cereal and milk, fruit and yogurt. But the real reason they were there was that the cafeteria was a good place to have a Dregg Dash, where people could race their Dreggs. Glowie could now do a sidestepping movement that Nory called "doing the grapevine," and she was fast. Nory couldn't wait to pit her against Elliott's Grog Dragon, who could now turn cartwheels like a fiend.

Nory had instructed all the UDM kids to show up early, as well as Zinnia and the kids from kittenball, *if* they'd bought Dreggs like they'd said they would.

"Hey, everybody," Nory cried as she banged through the swinging doors of the cafeteria. "It's time for our first ever Dregg Dash!"

She stopped short. There were *a lot* of kids in the cafeteria. Nory had forgotten how many people would be there, just to eat breakfast.

Oh, well. They could watch the Dregg Dash! Breakfast entertainment!

She and Elliott cleared an aisle between tables. Andres waved at them from up on the ceiling, with Willa holding his leash. Bax, Pepper, and Sebastian came over, too.

"Is the Dregg Dash a race?" Pepper asked.

"Yup," Nory said.

"But Mudpie doesn't move," Pepper said. She held her Mud Dragon in her palm. "I mean, I love her. Don't get me wrong." Pepper stroked Mudpie's head. "She's learned to turn herself inside out and back again, but she does it while staying in the same place."

Mudpie squeaked and retracted her head like a turtle. Then Mudpie's head disappeared entirely, swallowed by her inside-out-ing body, which popped and twitched when the process was done. Mudpie's insides (now outside) were bright yellow. She looked a bit like a tennis ball.

Marigold joined the group. "Tootsie's no good at racing either," she said. "Unless she figures out a way to motor herself along using fart power." Tootsie lifted her tail and farted on command.

Nory felt warm as she looked at her friends' happy faces. She had done this. With the Dreggs. She'd brought her friends together! And if racing wasn't going to work, she'd look at the bright side. "The Dregg Dash doesn't have to be a race," she said. "It can be, um, a circus-type thing, with all the Dreggs showing off. How's that?"

"Watch this!" cried a fifth-grade Flicker named Clyde. He elbowed his way into the group, his right hand clenched in a fist. "Make way!"

Nory was confused. She knew Clyde, but not

well. He was round, like a plum. His dark hair was super curly, more curly even than Nory's, and when he smiled, dimples flashed in the warm brown circle of his face.

Nory had nothing against Clyde. He seemed like a nice enough guy. He hadn't signed Lacey Clench's horrible petition against the UDM kids at the beginning of the school year. He'd never made fun of Nory and her friends in the halls. But why was he barging in now, acting all important?

A long, loud farting sound busted out from between Clyde's fingers.

Ooooooh.

Clyde beamed and opened his hand, revealing a freshly hatched, bright orange dragon. A tiny Tangerine Dragon!

"Great Dregg," Nory said, trying to shove away a surge of envy. On the UDM field trip last month, she and her friends had seen Tangerine Dragons at a dragon rescue and rehabilitation center. The real live

Tangerines were huge. They loved eating cantaloupes. This was the first Tangerine Dregg she'd seen.

"Check it out," Clyde said, digging around in his pocket. "Tangerine Dragons love fruit. And look what Juice-Juice does."

He withdrew a small red box of raisins. "Gobble up, Juice-Juice," he said, shaking two raisins onto the floor.

The tiny toy dragon walked over and ate a raisin. And then another.

"This particular Dregg cost a little extra," said Clyde. "It only eats raisins, though, and nothing else. I tried feeding it peanuts, but it wouldn't touch them."

Another Flicker kid came and sat down by Clyde. "Can I see?"

Then another Flicker came over. And another.

All the Flickers oohed and aahed over Juice-Juice and Tootsie and Mudpie. Paige, Finn, and Akari pulled out their new Dreggs to show, too. Their Fluxer friends clustered around, curious what was going on.

Nory put Glowie and Howler down in the aisle between the tables. Bax did the same with his dragon. So did Sebastian, Willa, Pepper, Elliott, and Marigold. Paige had another Luminous Dragonette. Akari had a Bumblebee Dragon, all yellow and black. Finn had a Seashell Dragon, a kind that Nory hadn't seen before.

Dreggs were hopping and rolling over. One sneezed a tiny sneeze. Another jumped high in the air. Glowie tap-danced, holding a pretzel stick like a cane. Other Dreggs walked on hind legs, or barked, or scratched their ears with their hind legs. Juice-Juice chased his tail.

It was a tiny Dregg circus!

"How about if all of you come to my house on Saturday?" Clyde said. "We can have a Dregg party!"

"Who does he mean?" Elliott whispered to Nory.

"Who do you mean?" Nory asked Clyde.

"All of you," Clyde confirmed, looking at the UDM kids, the Flickers with Dreggs, and the kitten-ballers. "Anyone with Dreggs."

Marigold grinned. "I'll be there."

Pepper grinned, too. "I can come, so long as you don't have any pets I might scare."

"No pets," said Clyde.

Most of the other kids said they could come, too, and Clyde told them to come at noon. "We can get pizza and do an even bigger Dregg Dash than this," he said cheerily.

It was five minutes until the school day officially began. The cafeteria workers began shooing the kids out. Time to go to class.

Nory sighed. She was glad to go to a party, but she didn't like Clyde barging in on the Dregg scene. He apparently had a big basement rec room and parents who didn't mind if he planned a party without even asking them first. Plus he had enough spending money to get an expensive Dregg that Nory didn't even know about, a Dregg that ate raisins. Actual raisins!

She couldn't hate Clyde. He was too nice. But sheesh, she wished he would just flicker himself invisible. And silent.

She herded her Dreggs back into their shells and put them in her backpack.

"Nory?" someone asked. It was Clyde.

"Yeah?"

"Can you help me? I can't get Juice-Juice back into his egg. I've tried four times. And I have to put him back because Ms. Applegate said she'll confiscate any dragon-shaped Dreggs if they come into her classroom."

"She really said that?"

"She really did," said Clyde.

"Can't you just turn Juice-Juice invisible? You're a Flicker, after all."

"My invisible things only stay invisible for like half an hour right now," Clyde said. "Not all day." He looked embarrassed. "I'm a little behind in Flicker studies."

Nory took hold of Clyde's tiny dragon and his eggshell. "Hmm," she said. "Hmm, hmm, hmm." She noted Juice-Juice's round, full belly. "I think he needs to poop. Then he'll fit back in his shell.

"Oh." Clyde furrowed his brow, then ripped a

napkin into shreds and piled the shreds together in the compartment of a lunch tray. He'd made an impromptu litter box.

"Go on, then," Nory said, gently urging Juice-Juice into the litter box. Juice-Juice scrunched his face and squatted. Out came a tiny purple plastic poop. Nory and Clyde looked at each other, and when Clyde laughed, Nory did, too. She couldn't help it.

After that, Juice-Juice hopped eagerly into his eggshell, and Clyde clicked the two halves together. "Sweet," he said. "Thanks. I'll see you on Saturday?"

"Sure," said Nory. She hadn't been sure till now that she wanted to go. "I'll be there."

In Ms. Starr's class, they were studying poetry. Every-one sat at their desks, and they were taking turns reading a very long, sad poem about the inky death of a giant squid who fought with a whale.

Every kid's Dregg was back in egg shape. And except for Andres, who floated on the ceiling, every kid's Dregg was on the corner of his or her desk.

Bax was reading aloud about the long tendrils of the sad and lonely squid when Nory saw Elliott squeeze his Dregg. Then she watched it hatch with a large farting noise. *Bluuuuuuuph!*

She laughed. *Everyone* laughed.

Groggy then stood up on his tiptoes and twirled, as if he were performing ballet.

Bax pressed the edges of his mouth together for a second, hard, and kept reading with a straight face.

Then Sebastian squeezed his Blurper Dragon Dregg and let it hatch. It started yodeling.

At this point, Bax completely lost it, laughing so hard he knocked his photocopy of the poem onto the floor.

Ms. Starr put her hands on her hips. "Friends. I need the toys put away. I was flexible this morning during roll call and morning announcements, but now that we are doing literature, I'm putting my foot down."

A couple of students put their Dreggs into pockets

and backpacks. But Pepper was still petting Mudpie. Mudpie purred. "More! More!" the tiny dragon squeaked.

"*Every*body, and I mean *now*!" snapped Ms. Starr.

Nory blinked, because Ms. Starr was a super-nice teacher. She wore brightly colored clothes and had a big braided bun on the top of her head. She stood up for her students and taught them hula-hooping and headstands and foot painting to help them balance their energies and make the most of their upside-down magic. She didn't usually get cross.

Pepper put Mudpie away. "Thank you," Ms. Starr said as everyone finally settled down. "All right, then. Willa, would you read aloud the next stanza?"

As Willa read, Nory felt a squirming in her hoodie pocket. Oh, no. Howler was hatching. She must have accidentally squeezed the egg.

"Very nice, Willa," said the teacher. You read with so much expression. Marigold, will you go next, please?"

Cr-ack. Nory felt it happen.

And then: *p-b-b-b-fffffffffl!*

Ms. Starr jumped to standing. Nory sank down in her seat. The class exploded in laughter.

Ms. Starr folded her arms. "Students. I understand that sometimes it is hard to tell if your toy is resting or if it is ready to hatch. I'm going to ask you all, please, to confirm that your toys are resting so that we can focus on this unhappy giant squid. When we are done reading, we are going discuss internal rhymes. Nory, will you read?"

Nory put Howler back into resting egg shape and read aloud a stanza of the poem.

But she couldn't help thinking that literature was more fun with Dreggs than it was without.

6

Marigold concentrated on her headstand. School would be through in less than an hour, and Ms. Starr was finishing the day by having everyone practicing being upside down. As she tried to keep from wobbling, Marigold thought about Clyde's party. She had said she'd go. But she was nervous. She had never been to Clyde's house. She and Clyde weren't friends.

In fact, Marigold wasn't friends with any typical kids except for Zinnia, because so many of the typical kids had been rude or mean about the UDM kids' talents. And with Marigold in particular, lots of the typical kids were scared of her. Earlier in the year she'd accidentally shrunk Lacey Clench down to the size of a gerbil.

Shrinking Lacey had been a huge mistake, but Marigold had lost her temper after Lacey mocked her hearing aids. Lacey had been taken to the hospital, where it took ten different shots to re-grow her to normal size. She'd had to drink eighteen glasses of coconut water to flush her system out.

Since then, things had gotten a bit better between the kids with typical magic and the kids with upside-down magic, but Marigold was still surprised to be invited to a party.

"Oh!" Ms. Starr exclaimed in a surprised voice. "Hello, Layla. Can I help you?"

Marigold opened her eyes. Layla stood in the doorway, breathing hard. "I'm here for Marigold," she said.

She met Marigold's gaze, and her eyes vibrated with electricity. Layla was a force of nature. Or maybe just extremely hyper.

"Come on, M-Boogie," she said. "I have fun stuff for us to do."

Marigold came out of her headstand.

"Hold on," Ms. Starr said. "Marigold, it's not your normal tutoring day."

"But I'm here," Layla said. "And since when does a UDM teacher care about *normal?*" She pushed back a chunk of her blue hair. "Please let her come. M-Boogie, I have a plan for you."

"Well . . . all right," Ms. Starr said.

"Aces," Layla said, giving Ms. Starr a thumbs-up.

In the hall, Layla didn't turn toward the library, where they'd met before. Instead, she led Marigold right *out the front door of the school.*

Marigold felt light-headed. "You got permission for me to leave school?"

Layla looked at her funny. "Don't worry. I'll get you back before the bell rings."

They walked down the block to the Daily Grind, a cute coffeehouse. Inside, they sat on an old-fashioned couch with wood trim and velvet upholstery. The menu was posted on a chalkboard above the counter. People were reading and working on laptop computers. It was so grown-up!

"What can I get you?" Layla asked.

"Chocolate milk, please," Marigold said, looking at the menu. Then she felt silly for choosing something babyish. "I mean, um, hot chocolate. With coffee? That's a thing you can get, isn't it?"

Layla nodded. "That's a mocha latte. One sec. My treat."

She returned with a large steaming drink for Marigold and a very small ceramic cup filled with black stuff for herself. She saw Marigold's expression and said, "Espresso." She took a sip from the teeny cup.

Marigold had never drunk coffee before, except little taster sips. Here was her own coffee drink. Would it be terrible?

Phew. It was delicious. Sweet and creamy, with a pretty white milk foam on top.

"What's your plan for me?" she asked Layla.

Layla took another sip of her espresso, then leaned forward across the table. "In the last few years, I've done a ton of research on the magic of making things big and small," she said. "Usually it's Fluxer magic. Fluxers always change size when they flux, right?"

"Right."

"But the bigger the size change, the harder it is, and the more unusual. Lots of people do house cats. Almost all Fluxers do. And that does involve getting smaller. But very few people do bugs. They're just soooo tiny. And it's more common for people to big up than shrink down to the really small sizes. Elephant Fluxers aren't actually that unusual. Or rhinos. All those tigerball players can do tigers, and some of them weigh six hundred and fifty pounds. It's a tough flux, but not exactly rare."

"My friend Nory can do mosquito and elephant," said Marigold. "Well, only mixed up with other animals. But she can do them."

"Then she's a super-rare Fluxer," said Layla. "Most people do medium-sized animals, and they only go really big or really small, but not both. Tigerball players don't do caterpillars. People's natural talent is usually for one or the other. Anyway. My own magic has always been labeled upside down without a category, like yours. But in grad school, I had a revelation. I'm a Fluxer! Just, I don't do any animals. Instead I just flux my own body."

"Oh, cool," said Marigold.

"I can make myself big or I can make myself small. Take, for example, my foot." At this, Layla's foot (and the sneaker it wore) became enormous. Then it shrank down to the size of a doll foot, while the rest of her leg remained normal size, starting at the ankle.

"Or I can make my hands big or small, whatever I like. I can grow my nose if I want it longer, or my hair." Layla's short blue hair thickened and stretched out all the way to her waist, where it remained. "And I can sustain it. But it takes effort, just like fluxing does. Fluxers don't stay in animal shapes all day, just the way Flyers don't stay up in the air all the time. Too much work."

"Totally."

"But my magic is different from fluxing in one key way: I can affect *other people's bodies*. I can big them up or shrink them, whereas typical Fluxers can't do anything to other people's bodies. Now, think. Which of the five Fs *can* do things to other people's bodies?"

"Flickers," answered Marigold. "And certain Flyers."

"Well done. Flickers can turn a variety of things invisible. Small animals, objects, buildings, even other people." Layla gave a nod. "So there's a way my magic is related to flickering as well."

"I think I have fitting magic," Marigold said. "Not one of the five Fs at all. I fit things to a different size."

"You're an original thinker, kid. I like it," said Layla. "I've studied other kinds of size-changing magic. Some of them don't seem to be fluxing and flickering at all."

Marigold smiled. Layla took her seriously!

"Now," said Layla, "I dug into some of my notebooks

(55)

this morning, and I think I found a technique for bigging up that might work for you. Not the same as what I do. More related to some of those rarer size-changing magics. Let me be sure I understand: You can shrink, but you can't big up. And you shrink things by accident sometimes, right?"

"Right. Though I do it less than I used to, because of studying upside-down magic techniques with Ms. Starr," said Marigold.

"Thatta girl. Now, I want you to take a picture of yourself in your mind. Make it a picture of your whole body, cool clothes and all. Taking up space. Being awesome. Okay?"

"Okay." Marigold took a mental snapshot of herself.

"Now," said Layla, "we need to choose something to big up." She took another sip of her espresso and looked around. She grabbed the heavy hoodie Marigold had been wearing under her jacket. "Perfect. We'll big this up. Add the hoodie to your mental snapshot and then enlarge the snapshot in your head. We do it on computers all the time, right? We make something bigger. So you can do it in your head. Give it a shot!"

"Should I enlarge the whole snapshot, me included?" Marigold asked. "Or just the hoodie?"

"Oh, right. Just the hoodie." Layla rolled her fingers to say *Go on, then.*

Marigold did. In her mind she made the hoodie bigger than everything else in her mental snapshot. Her head began to tingle and her fingers began to buzz, the way they did before she shrank something.

"Okay, now. When you shrink things, you let the magic out of your fingers, right?"

"Yes."

"When you big up, you're going to let this big snapshot zwoop out your forehead. Like a bubble. Okay?"

Marigold imagined the big snapshot as a bubble, ready to burst. She directed the bubble and imagined throwing it hard. *Zwoop!*

"M-Boogie! You did it!" Layla cried.

The tingling in Marigold's head and fingers stopped. She looked at the sweatshirt. The sleeves were definitely longer. It looked bulkier, too. She hadn't bigged it up a ton, but she had bigged it. She really had!

"Excellent," Layla said. "I mean, seriously. I am amazing." She grabbed Marigold's hand. "And you are, too. You bigged something up, M-Boogie." Layla jumped up. "Major progress today, right? Okay. I gotta motor." She tossed back the last of her espresso. "I'll see you next week. You can make it back to school on your own, right?"

Marigold nodded.

"Rock on. Keep practicing. But only on objects. Don't big up anything alive until I teach you. And call me anytime if you have problems. Always happy to help."

Layla left.

Marigold realized she didn't have Layla's number.

The café seemed suddenly empty. Marigold looked around. People were still reading their books and working on their laptops. She took a few sips of her mocha and glowed.

She could big up. There had been a change in her magic!

Finally, she stood and put on the sweatshirt, then her jacket. As she walked back to school, she pulled the long sleeves of the bigged-up sweatshirt over her hands, turning them into mittens.

School was letting out when Marigold returned. Everyone poured out of the building and into the chilly afternoon.

"We're going to get the bus to Brilliant Ned's so we can buy more Dreggs," Willa said, stopping to catch Marigold's arm. "Everyone's going. Want to come? I have some money. Ooh!" Willa squealed, looking at Marigold's sweatshirt sleeves. "Did you make that bigger? At your tutoring?"

"I bigged it up," Marigold said.

"Wow!" Willa hugged Marigold. "That's a huge step with your magic. I'm so happy for you."

Marigold was happy, too. They linked arms and headed off to Brilliant Ned's.

7

At noon on Saturday, Nory, Elliott, Willa, and Marigold arrived at Clyde's party. Nory felt shy as she rang the doorbell. She was glad she had her UDM friends with her.

By now, practically everyone in the fifth grade had a Dregg. The Flickers. The Flyers. The Fluxers. The Fuzzies. And all the Flares. Lacey Clench had ten Dreggs. Ten!

Lunch on Friday had been crazy, in a good way. Everyone had taken out their Dreggs as soon as they'd sat down to eat. Dreggs were sitting on people's pizza slices, hopping on juice boxes, shaking themselves like wet dogs when they stepped in spilled milk.

After that, kids got their Dreggs wet on purpose. Elliott poured his apple juice on Groggy, and Groggy danced around like he was singing in the rain. Pepper poured milk on Mudpie, and Mudpie pretended to lap it up.

Soon the UDM table, and then the Flicker table, and then nearly every table in the cafeteria was covered with liquid. Willa made a tiny rain cloud over her pale green Grass Dragon and the other kids put their sticky little dragons under the cloud to rinse off, rubbing them gently with paper napkins. Most of the dragons seemed to like that, but Andres's Buttress Dragon cried.

"Aw, you're okay," Andres cooed, toweling off his dragon. To the others, he said, "She doesn't like baths, that's all. She's fine."

Anyway. The lunch workers put a stop to everything eventually. They made the kids help clean up the spilled juice and milk. Willa got scolded for her rain cloud, even though it had helped everyone clean their Dreggs.

Outside for recess, the kids whooshed their dragons down the slides and pushed them in the swings. The UDM kids dug a pit in the yard where the Dreggs could roll in dirt. It was mud mania.

Then nearly everyone had gone as a group to Brilliant Ned's and bought more Dreggs so they'd have new dragons to hatch at Clyde's party.

And now it was party time.

Clyde threw open the door and smiled. "Come in, come in," he called. Nory and the others followed him as he jogged down a set of stairs. "The party's in the rec room. Zinnia's already here. So are Talon and Rainey. Do you all know Talon and Rainey?"

Nory knew who they were—Flicker friends of Clyde's. Talon was a short boy. Rainey was a tall non-binary kid. Both wore sweatshirts and brightly colored sneakers. But Nory didn't *really know* them. Yeah, they had never been actively mean to the UDM kids, but they'd never been actively nice, either. They hung around with other Flickers and played soccer at recess. Also, Flickers made Nory nervous. They were known for practical jokes. They'd turn your food invisible, turn your backpack invisible, even turn *you* invisible and shove you in a locker.

Would Talon and Rainey call Nory and her friends *wonkos* and play tricks on them?

No, she told herself. They would be nice.

Clyde was nice, right?

The basement rec room had been decorated with streamers and glitter strings and balloons. There were bowls of potato chips and choco fire trucks and jugs of what looked like lemonade. Talon and Rainey were eating potato chips and talking to Zinnia.

Nory ran over to Zinnia. "Did you bring your new Dreggs?"

Zinnia nodded. Everyone had spent their saved money at Brilliant Ned's. Each kid had at least two Dreggs, and some people had lots.

Clyde had set up Dregg activity stations all over the basement: a mini trampoline where Dreggs could bounce, an old toddler slide that Dreggs could go down, and a Dregg obstacle course made with Dixie cups and bungee cords. He had a tape measure spread out on the floor to measure how far each Dregg could hop.

Nory's favorite Dregg was still Glowie. Glowie was truly awesome on the trampoline. She and Elliott made Glowie and Groggy bounce insanely high. Marigold's new Sparkle Dragon, Sparkle-Puff, could bounce pretty high, too. He did somersaults in the air.

Ten minutes later, the room was full of kids, typicals and non-typicals alike. Clyde, Talon, and Andres, who wore his backpack full of bricks, measured how far their Dreggs could jump. Paige, Pepper, and Zinnia giggled as their Dreggs slid down the tiny slide. Willa and Marigold sat on a couch, urging their Dreggs back into the eggs so they could re-hatch them.

"This is a good party," Nory said to Elliott.

Elliott smiled. "I didn't want to tell you before, but I was nervous."

"I was, too," said Nory.

They ate potato chips. They drank lemonade. None of the Flickers did anything mean. None of the UDM kids did anything embarrassing. At one point, they herded six Dreggs onto the trampoline at once and got them all to bounce together.

Paige, Akari, and Finn fluxed into kittens for a bit, playing with the Dreggs and batting them with their paws. Nory was tempted to flux with them, but she did still sometimes accidentally add dragon or goat or mosquito to her kitten, and she didn't want to risk damaging Clyde's decorations or his kind of fancy furniture by losing control of her human mind. So she just stayed Girl-Nory and had a good time.

At four thirty, Clyde's dad brought down a chocolate layer cake. He was handing out slices when Sebastian appeared. As usual, he wore his special aviator goggles to keep the noises in the loud room from overwhelming his sensitive eyeballs.

The UDM kids waved at him. "Finally!" said Elliott.

"Sorry, sorry," Sebastian said. He said hello to Clyde and accepted a slice of cake, but instead of joining the festivities, he came up to Nory and told her they had to talk, right that instant.

"It's about Dreggs," he said.

"Yeah, you missed the games, slowpoke. But everything's still set up. I bet you can get people to play."

"No, no," Sebastian said. "The Dreggs have been banned. Principal Gonzalez sent an email to all the parents. Dreggs are banned at Dunwiddle from now until forever!"

"Banned?" It was so unfair. Why would Principal Gonzalez do that? Nory waved her hands to get the others' attention. "Listen to Sebastian, everyone. He has bad news."

The room went silent, and Sebastian explained.

Then everyone spoke at once.

"No Dreggs at school?" cried Rainey. They sank into a chair, distraught.

Finn kicked the carpet. "Why do they have to ruin our fun? Dreggs never hurt anyone."

"Exactly," Clyde said.

Dreggs banned at school? No, no, no. It was a horrible idea. Nory vowed to fight back.

8

Marigold was really glad she'd come to Clyde's party. She loved how Sparkle-Puff was showing off his new tricks. Sparkle-Puff was special. Sparkle Dragons were flexible, athletic river dragons, so Sparkle-Puff was more flexible than any of the other Dreggs. He could contort himself into all kinds of catlike positions, and had the cutest little webbed feet. He jumped really high as well.

When Sebastian showed up and broke the bad news about the Dregg ban, Marigold was bummed.

She didn't think it was fair for the school to ban something that brought kids so much happiness.

Her granddad arrived as things were breaking up. He was collecting Willa, too, and taking them both out to dinner.

Marigold and Willa both made their farewells and thanked Clyde and his parents for the party.

"How was everything?" asked Granddad Lorenzo as they walked to the center of town.

"Zwingo," said Marigold. "It was fun."

"I used to host parties a lot when I was your age," said Granddad Lorenzo. "The whole neighborhood came over. My mom would make tortillas and we'd all eat tacos sitting in the backyard. And your grandmother and I had a lot of parties when we first got married, too. She had a pot to make chocolate fondue."

"I want to make chocolate fondue," said Marigold. "Wait. What is it?"

"It's a pot of melted chocolate that stays warm with a little flame under it. You spear things on skewers and dip them in the chocolate," explained Granddad Lorenzo. "Pound cake, bananas, straw-berries. Should we get Grandmom to search for the fondue pot?"

"Yes," cried Marigold, feeling bouncy.

She and Willa linked arms and walked ahead of Granddad in the fading light.

The restaurant was lit with candles and had a small fountain in the entryway. Willa, Granddad, and Marigold were given hot washcloths to clean their hands. They ordered dumplings and cucumber rolls and edamame. The waiter came and lit a candle in the center of their table.

"Let's hear about your tutor on Friday," said Granddad Lorenzo. He was a Fuzzy and worked with the dogs who helped the Dunwiddle police force, keeping the animals healthy and taking them out to do their police jobs.

"Layla is super unusual," Marigold said slowly. "Like, she doesn't believe in rules."

"Really? But rules keep our society together. Don't they?" asked Granddad Lorenzo.

"I'm not sure," Marigold said. "Like what about the new 'No Dreggs' rule?" She stopped and made sure Granddad had seen the email. He had, so she went on. "It wasn't a rule, and now it is. *Kaboom.* I wonder: All Principal Gonzalez had to do was write one single email? That's all it takes to make a rule that affects hundreds of kids?"

Willa squinted. "When you put it like that . . . zamboozle."

The food arrived. "Does Willa know about bigging up your sweatshirt?" Granddad Lorenzo asked Marigold.

"Of course."

"Marigold's been practicing a lot at home," Granddad told Willa. "She bigged up several things. The fruit was the most fun."

Marigold smiled. "I made jumbo grapes and jumbo raspberries."

"How big?" asked Willa.

"Not *that* big," said Marigold. "Not as big as your head or anything."

"They were definitely bigger than usual," said Granddad. "They were the size of apples."

"The raspberries went mushy before we could eat them all," said Marigold.

"But it's an ingenious way to save money," said Granddad. "Bigging up your groceries. We're very excited about that."

Marigold blushed. It was true. It was the first time her magic had been *useful*.

"Bigging up the toothbrushes wasn't such a success," continued Granddad.

"No," Marigold added. "And bigging up the pillows on the couch just made them look weird."

"Couldn't you shrink them again?" asked Willa.

"I had trouble re-shrinking the pillows. Maybe I need to practice moving between shrinking and bigging up? I don't know why, but it's hard to switch back and forth."

"Jumbo couch pillows won't hurt us any," said Granddad. "And I'm looking forward to saving on my grocery bill."

"Can you show me the bigging up?" asked Willa. "Please?"

Marigold looked around the restaurant. She focused on one lone dumpling, uneaten on Willa's plate. She made the snapshot of herself in her mind. Then she enlarged it until her forehead tingled and *zwoop*!

"Marigold!" Willa cried, laughing. "That is awesome." The dumpling now dwarfed the plate. It was the size of a large watermelon! It slopped all over the tablecloth and glopped itself on top of the candle, putting out the flame.

Marigold was surprised at how big the dumpling had gotten. At home, she had been making things a *bit* bigger, but not huge. She'd expected the dumpling to grow to the size of an apple, like the grapes had.

Granddad Lorenzo looked around. "Marigold, that's a lot for the waitstaff to clean up," he whispered.

"It's all greasy. I'm really glad you can big things up, honey, but it would be great if you could shrink the dumpling back down."

Marigold flushed. "Of course. I didn't mean for it to get that big."

Some other diners were looking over. Marigold shook her hands out and tried to just think casually about shrinking, the way she always had. She scrunched her face and aimed her fingers at the jumbo dumpling.

Zwoop!

Nothing happened. Willa's eyes grew big. "Try again, Marigold."

Marigold tried to shrink the dumpling again.

No luck.

"Granddad, I'm sorry," she whispered. "I just can't shrink it."

Granddad wrinkled his brow. Then he smiled. "I have a tote bag in my coat pocket," he said, pulling out a folded canvas bag. He held the bag open beneath the table, and Willa and Marigold pushed the jumbo dumpling in.

"Well, I guess I know what I'm having for lunch tomorrow," Grandad said with a laugh. Willa laughed, too.

Marigold didn't find it funny. If she couldn't fix her mistakes, her magic wasn't that useful after all.

9

On Monday morning, Nory woke up feeling different. She had thought about it all day Sunday, and she'd come to a decision.

Ban or no ban, she was bringing her Dreggs to school.

That Principal Gonzalez. Who did he think he was, making rules about kids' toys?! Nory could understand Ms. Starr asking kids to put Dreggs away while she was teaching. That, at least, made sense. But banning the Dreggs from recess? And the lunchroom?

It was just. Too. Much.

If Nory didn't bring her Dreggs to school with her, they would suffer. Without the proper amount of attention, they'd learn no new tricks. She wouldn't be doing right by her Dreggs.

So she was bringing them. Done. No one would stop her. No one *could* stop her! She would be sneaky about it.

In Ms. Starr's classroom, everything was just like it always was. Willa whispered happily with Marigold and didn't rain on anyone. Bax was his usual sullen self, twirling a pencil in his hands. Andres wore his brickpack and sat in his seat. Ms. Starr's companion rabbit, Carrot, sat cheerfully on the teacher's desk, munching on a slice of apple.

Carrot was immune to Pepper's scary magic. She could also talk, thanks to Ms. Starr's upside-down magic, which gave speech to animals. "Good morning," the bunny said to each kid on arrival. "How was your weekend? Ms. Starr and I went apple picking."

Nory couldn't be bothered with Carrot, not today. She was too busy thinking about injustice.

After taking roll and making morning announcements—including an announcement about the Dregg ban—Ms. Starr dimmed the lights. She began a science lecture with slides on the big screen. The fifth graders had finished their unit on dragons and were now learning about volcanoes. Carrot went to sleep in the top drawer of Ms. Starr's desk. She liked the kids, but she didn't care much for lessons.

Nory slipped her hand into her backpack and brought out Glowie's egg. She wouldn't hatch Glowie, not in class. Of course not. She would just hold the egg. Nobody would know. And maybe it would count as playing. Maybe Glowie-in-her-egg could tell the egg was being held? Maybe it would help her learn.

Behind Nory, Bax repositioned his chair, the metal legs scraping loudly on the floor. The sound startled Nory, and her fingers clenched reflexively around the Dregg. *Squeeze!*

Uh-oh. She hadn't meant to squeeze it.

Ms. Starr kept talking about magma. She showed a video of glowing red lava spraying all over the place.

Glowie-in-her-egg wobbled and rocked.

P-b-b-bbbbbbh! Glowie hatched.

The bitsy dragon popped out of Nory's hand and bounced onto the floor, where she rolled several times, then picked herself up and shook herself like a wet dog.

Elliott giggled. So did Bax. So did Marigold. Soon the whole class was laughing.

Ms. Starr rapped her knuckles on her desk. "Friends. What's so funny?"

"Mrp!" Glowie chirped.

The dragon hopped forward and crashed into the leg of Elliott's desk, which was next to Nory's. Then she fell over and played dead, with all four feet up in the air. Andres fell out of his seat, he was laughing so hard. He squirmed out of his brickpack and floated to the ceiling.

Pepper covered her face with her hands, her

shoulders shaking. Ms. Starr narrowed her eyes and flicked on the lights. She marched over to Elliott's desk and looked underneath it.

Uh-oh.

The teacher picked up the toy dragon. "Whose Dregg is this?"

No one answered.

"Elliott?" Ms. Starr loomed over him.

"It's not mine."

"It's under your desk."

"It . . ." Elliott looked like he was about to tell on Nory, but he clamped his mouth shut.

"Elliott, I want you to tell me the truth," said the teacher. "You know these toys are not allowed at school."

Elliott kept his mouth shut.

Oh, drat. Nory couldn't let Elliott get in trouble because of her Dregg.

"Glowie's mine," she told Ms. Starr. "Sorry."

Ms. Starr looked really and truly mad. She held up the dragon and took the Dregg shell off Nory's desk. She popped Glowie back into the egg. "Thank you for speaking up, Nory. As for this, it belongs to me now, until I can speak to Principal Gonzalez."

"What?" Nory exclaimed. "No way. *Ms. Starr!*"

Surely Ms. Starr wasn't really against Dreggs. She was the nicest teacher ever!

But Ms. Starr's gaze was steely. She opened her bottom desk drawer, dropped the Dregg inside, and closed the drawer with a resounding bang.

"It is my right to take away contraband, and that is exactly what I will do to any Dregg I see in this classroom. *Or* on the playground. *Or* in the cafeteria." Ms. Starr surveyed the class. "Is that understood?"

Nory simmered. Yes, it was understood. But Nory didn't accept it. Ms. Starr didn't understand. If you left your Dreggs at home, you weren't doing right by them.

It was time to rebel, and Nory would happily lead the rebellion.

10

Marigold was both shocked and impressed that Nory had brought her Dregg to school. Apparently some of the Flickers had done the same thing. She heard about it at recess. The teachers had confiscated Juice-Juice and several others.

Marigold had hated leaving Sparkle-Puff and Tootsie back at home. Especially Sparkle-Puff. All day, she missed the way he contorted himself into the funniest positions, how he leapt in the air when he was surprised. She loved how he made her smile, and the way people clustered around her to see what Sparkle-Puff was doing next. The splits. A backbend!

She also missed everyone playing with their Dreggs together. She had never been part of something like that before. The party. The Dregg Dash in the cafeteria. It was wonderful.

Maybe she could invite some of her friends over after school for another Dregg Dash?

The day felt dull and boring without Dreggs.

When Layla showed up for her afternoon tutoring session, Marigold was happy for the distraction. "Come on, M-Boogie, let's do this thing," Layla said. "Today is going to be awesome."

Marigold expected them to go to the library, or maybe to the coffee shop, but this time, Layla walked out to the schoolyard. The two of them sat next to each other on swings. It was too late in the day for anyone to be at recess.

Layla pumped her legs and swung up high. Marigold swung, too.

"All right, kiddo," Layla said. "The method I

taught you for bigging things up allows your magic to work through your hands and forehead, yes? Shrinking things with your hands, bigging things up with your head?"

"Yes." Marigold glowed. Layla was so smart.

"Okay, cool. So we've got that part figured out: You use your hands to shrink and your forehead to big up. How's it going? Did you practice?"

"I did, and some parts of it are good," Marigold said. "But I'm still having trouble."

"What's wrong?" asked Layla.

Marigold explained about the fruit and the toothbrushes and couch pillows. "Of course I'm really happy about finally being able to make stuff big. Especially the fruit. I just wish I had more control over my magic." She told the story of the jumbo dumpling.

"Wow."

"It upset my granddad. And the waitstaff would have had to deal with it if we hadn't had a tote bag with us."

Layla slowed her swing. "Listen. You don't have to

let other people's opinions bother you, Marigold. You could just be proud that you made a giant dumpling."

"That's not it. What bothers me is that I always used to be able to shrink things whenever I wanted."

Layla nodded thoughtfully. Then she hopped off the swing and grabbed a basketball lying in the fly-ball court. "Grow this."

Marigold bigged up the basketball, just a bit.

"Bigger!" said Layla.

Marigold put a little more power behind it, and the basketball became the size of an extra-large pumpkin. Hurrah!

Layla enlarged herself, just like she had that day in the library, and dribbled the big basketball from one end of the fly-ball court to the other in five strides.

Then she blinked hard and shrank back to her usual size. She rested her arm on top of the basketball and grinned. "I, personally, appreciate this giant basketball."

"Coach might not," Marigold said. "He's the PE teacher."

"All right, well, let's see if you can shrink it."

Marigold tried. The basketball stayed big.

"Could it be a timing problem?" she asked Layla. "Like, maybe I can't shrink something if I've just bigged it up. Maybe there's too much, um, left-over bigging magic. Could that be it?"

"Let's explore that idea," said Layla. "Shrink the swing set."

"Will you re-grow it if I can't?"

"Maybe it would be better if you figured out how to do it yourself."

"Yeah, but what if I can't? I don't want everyone to be upset with me."

"Who cares what they think?" said Layla.

"I'll shrink this stick," said Marigold, picking one up from the ground.

She didn't need to think about the snapshot of herself to shrink it. Her fingers and head tingled, and *zwoop!* The stick was the size of her finger. Marigold was pleased to find she had stopped it at just the size she'd meant to. That wasn't something she could have done at the start of the school year.

"Nice tiny stick," said Layla. "And now we know that you *can* shrink right after bigging up. No rest time needed. So the problem must be shrinking what you've just bigged."

"Should I try to big it back up?" asked Marigold.

"Sure," said Layla.

Marigold put her fingertips to her temple and concentrated.

Nothing happened.

She tried again.

Nothing happened.

"I think if you're bigging up something you just shrank, you have to treat it differently," said Layla. "Imagine it like you normally would. Enlarge it in your head like you normally would. But use a gentler touch. Don't *force* the stick to grow bigger. *Coax* it, like maybe it's a little scared. It helps to think of objects you're working with as alive even though they're not. Flickers learn that when they study how to turn things invisible. They call it learning to coax."

Marigold concentrated. She enlarged her imaginary snapshot and she tried to coax the stick at the same time. *Zwoop!* She managed to make the stick go back to its normal size.

Hurrah!

Layla whooped. "Let's do more!" she cried.

The rest of the lesson went well. Layla taught Marigold some more Flicker techniques of coaxing. They shrank and then regrew a water bottle, a necklace, and a used tissue Layla dug out of her pocket. Finally, Marigold shrank the basketball back to its normal size. Success!

What a relief. Now if Marigold shrank something by accident, she would be able to bring it back to normal again. It was a real breakthrough. She planned to go to Mr. Wang in the library and make his books big again, right after school.

"We're done for today," Layla said, reaching out to

give Marigold a high five. "Could we be more awesome? I think not."

The two of them headed back to Ms. Starr's room. When they reached the door, Nory stormed out, holding a bathroom pass. Her brow was furrowed and she stopped in front of Marigold. "I'm so mad!" Nory said. "I don't even have to use the bathroom. I just had to get out of that classroom."

Then she turned into a dritten, blew a small amount of fire down the hallway, dropped the bathroom pass, and flew off in the direction of the restrooms.

Layla whistled. "That kid has some impressive magic. What's she so mad about?"

Marigold explained about the Dreggs and the new ban. Plus what had happened this morning, with Nory getting her Dregg taken away. "It's really unfair," said Marigold. "It's like, the teachers have all the power. They even get to decide how we play."

As Marigold talked, Layla made comments like

"No way" and "Are you kidding me right now?" and "Okay, omigosh, I cannot *even*."

"Nory's hosting an emergency after-school meeting today to talk about ways of fighting back," Marigold said. "She passed around notes during literature."

"Sweet," said Layla. "You kids have more power than you realize. I mean, if the Dreggs really are important to you, definitely make your opinion heard."

"But how?"

Layla slung one arm around Marigold, pulled her close, and drove her knuckles into Marigold's scalp. Marigold felt a bit like a puppy. "Protesting is a way of raising your voice," Layla said. "Last month, I organized a walkout of my whole Magical Studies Department. Of the grad students, anyway. We were fighting for fair payment for the teaching assistants, you know?"

Marigold nodded.

"The cool thing was, it started out with just four

of us. We thought nobody else cared. And maybe it wouldn't work. But once the four of us walked out, other people walked out. Soon there were no students in the department. And that's why the assistants got their raise." Layla pointed at Marigold. "You guys can raise your voices, too. Yeah, you're fighting for a toy, not a major social issue, but you still can find a way to say what's important to you. Speak up if you don't think the rule is fair."

"For sure," Marigold said.

"Thatta girl."

11

Only Marigold, Willa, and Elliott showed up for Nory's protest meeting. Other people had after-school lessons or club meetings. Still, Aunt Margo's kitchen felt crowded, because everyone brought their Dreggs. Dreggs waddled among the bowls of chips and pretzels Nory had put on the counters. Dreggs trotted across the table and hopped on the spice rack. They toddled across the floor. Willa, Elliott, and Marigold sat on the floor patting and tickling them. Their Dreggs had been closed up all day while they were at school, so they had probably missed learning tricks.

"People?" Nory said loudly. "People. This is an important meeting, not a Dregg Dash."

Miraculously, Elliott and Willa and Marigold fell silent.

"You guys," Nory said. "As you know, Glowie has been confiscated. I didn't even get to take her home at the end of the day. The school is making rules about how we can play, even during recess. It isn't fair. We have to plan our protest. Does anyone have ideas?"

"Could we yell?" asked Elliott. "All of us yell, all day?"

"I think we'd get hoarse," said Marigold.

"Excuse me," said Willa. "What is our point with this protest, exactly? What are we trying to make happen?"

Nory explained. "Our point is that we should be allowed to bring our Dreggs to school, and that they're *not*—Marigold, could you please egg up Tootsie so she stops farting while I'm talking—they're not disruptive. If we yelled all day, like Elliott says, we would really be letting people know how mad we are. And the yelling would show them what's *really* disruptive."

Willa shook her head. "I don't think that would make Principal Gonzalez give us our Dreggs back. I think he would just tell us to be quiet."

"How about a Fart-a-Thon!" Elliott said. "That would make the teachers pay attention!"

"No one can fart on demand *all day*," Nory said. "I think we have to do something the teachers can't ignore. Something that makes them take us seriously."

"I think they'd take a Fart-a-Thon seriously," Elliott argued.

Marigold didn't seem to be paying attention, Nory noticed. With Tootsie back in her shell, Marigold was amusing herself by shrinking a pretzel, then bigging it back to normal. Shrink, grow. Shrink, grow.

Instead of brainstorming ideas for the perfect

protest, she just kept shrinking and growing that one silly pretzel. It was—

Ooh, it was brilliant! Omigosh, yes! That was it! Nory clapped and bounced. "Marigold. You're amazing."

"Huh?"

"We *shrink* ourselves. Or rather, Marigold shrinks us. *Yes!*"

"I don't get it," Elliott said.

"The teachers can't ignore us if we're small," Nory said.

"Um, actually, small things are easy to ignore," Elliott said.

"No," Nory said. "People. We are going to hold a shrink-in. Not a Fart-a-Thon. A big, big shrink-in!" She turned to Marigold. "You can grow things back now, right?"

Marigold sat up a little taller. "Well, yeah. Layla taught me how to re-grow things after I shrink them."

"It's settled, then. Tomorrow we'll tell the other fifth graders the plan. Then, on Wednesday, we'll all meet up and SHRINK. Best protest ever!"

"I don't get it," Willa said.

"Me neither," said Elliott. "Being tiny would be super fun. But how is it a protest?"

"I think I understand," Marigold said slowly. "It's a protest, but a peaceful one. Yelling would be disruptive, and teachers could make us stop. Farting is—well, we're not farting. But if the whole fifth grade shrinks, the teachers can't ignore us, but we also haven't done anything wrong. They can't even make us stop. None of them have growing magic."

"But *you* do," Nory cried. "Let's have a round of applause for Marigold, shall we?"

She clapped, and the others joined in.

Marigold smiled. "Fine," she said. "The Big Shrink it is."

12

Nory felt like a hummingbird, all flutter-flutter. She was so excited, telling everyone she knew about the Big Shrink.

"Our small protest is going to be capital-*B* Big!" she told Bax on Tuesday during lunch.

Bax regarded her dourly. "Count me out," he said.

"What?" Nory said. "Why?"

"When I get stressed, I flux into a rock."

"Duh."

"Well, if I'm *small* and I get stressed, I might flux into a pebble."

Nory saw it in her mind: Bax as a pebble, kicked down Dunwiddle's halls. She hated to admit it, but that did sound dangerous. Nory knew Bax couldn't turn back into a boy without help from Nurse Riley. If he became a pebble, he could skid into a crack and be lost forever.

Andres turned Nory down, too. He was afraid that if he turned tiny and somehow floated into the air, he'd disappear as easily as a dust mote or a puff of cat hair. "It's a cool idea, and it does sound fun, and I'll help out if you need me to. But as regular-sized me, not tiny me."

"Fine," Nory said. "I get it."

"I'm sorry to let you down, but I'm sure you'll get tons of other kids to say yes," Andres said.

Nory tried not to feel disheartened. She continued flitting from fifth grader to fifth grader, though with slightly less hummingbird energy than before. Some kids said no. Some said maybe. Lots of kids scratched their heads and looked skeptical, but Nory told herself that those kids *could* end up being yeses.

At least Elliott, Pepper, Sebastian, Willa, and Marigold were locked in. If they each recruited ten more people, that would be a lot of protesters.

"Tomorrow morning, fifteen minutes before school starts, by the invisible water fountain," she said over and over. "Be there and help us show the administration they shouldn't ban Dreggs. It's not fair for them to dictate what we play with in our free time."

When Wednesday finally arrived, Nory stood anxiously by the fountain. She held a sign she'd made over her head that read THE BIG SHRINK. Elliott had a clipboard for writing down the names of the kids who came. That way Marigold could make sure to big up every one she'd made small.

They waited.

And waited.

"Good morning, wonkos," said Lacey Clench, strolling up with Zinnia.

What? There was no way Lacey Clench was joining their protest. Was there?

Lacey was easily Nory's least favorite person at

Dunwiddle. Still, Nory lifted her chin and said, "Thanks for coming. We'll give the others another minute to get here, and then we'll start."

Lacey cleared her throat. "I'm only here to give moral support. Zinnia told me what you guys are doing and I do agree that banning Dreggs is stupid. My dad took me to Brilliant Ned's last night, and I bought four Dregg assortment packs. Each pack has ten Dreggs in it, which means I now have forty Dreggs."

"Gee, thanks for the math lesson," Nory said.

"Actually, forty new Dreggs plus the two I already had makes forty-two Dreggs."

"Whoop-dee-doo."

"I am all about Dreggs," Lacey pronounced. "Obviously." She turned to Marigold. "But don't shrink me. Been there, done that, don't want to experience it again."

"She can grow you back this time, though," Willa told Lacey. "You wouldn't have to go back to the hospital."

Lacey pursed her lips. "There is no way I'm going through that again, thank you very much." She rolled her hand in the air. "But please, proceed."

Clyde jogged up, flushed and out of breath. "Sorry I'm late, but I'm here now." He glanced around. "Is this all of us?"

"Oh, no," Nory said. "I'm expecting thirty more people at least."

"Just because you're expecting them doesn't mean they'll magically appear," Lacey noted.

Marigold tapped Nory's arm. "I think Lacey might be right," she said. "It's ten minutes after we said we'd meet, so this might be all of us. And we better start if we want to do this thing before the bell rings."

"But we need lots of people to shrink in order to make a good protest," Nory wailed.

"Layla did a small protest at her school," said Marigold. "And it ended up working. Other people saw her protesting and they joined in."

Nory sighed and looked on the bright side.

Marigold was right. It could still be awesome. "Okay, then. Is everyone ready?"

"Is this going to hurt?" Zinnia asked.

They all turned to Lacey.

"It didn't hurt," she admitted. "It was just super annoying."

"How tiny will we be?" Zinnia pressed.

"Three inches tall," said Marigold. "About the size of a gerbil on its hind legs."

"What if we get lost?"

"If you get separated from the group, or you need help, come wait here, by the invisible water fountain. We have Lacey, Andres, and Bax looking out for us."

"Okay," said Zinnia. "I'm in."

They all agreed.

Marigold locked eyes with Nory. "I'm ready. You're good to go?"

Nory puffed up, pleased that Marigold recognized her as the group's leader. "For sure," she said, grinning. "Let the Big Shrink begin!"

13

Marigold allowed herself only a moment's hesitation. She took a deep breath, summoned her magic, and felt the tingle in her hands.

Zwoop-plip-ploop! Nory, Elliott, Willa, Pepper, Sebastian, Zinnia, and Clyde—they shrank, one after the other. They were each now the height of a mouse, but not the width. Their bodies stayed proportional. They were teensy-tiny miniature versions of themselves.

And then, *zwoop!* Marigold was tiny, too. That

was the part she'd been worried about, but it worked like a charm.

"Whee!" she said, bouncing up and down. "I did it!"

"High five!" squeaked Elliott, slapping Marigold's palm.

"Zwingo!" cried Clyde.

"This is awesome," Sebastian said.

The air shattered around them as the first bell rang. The hall thundered with shoes and legs and noise and pants cuffs as kids poured out of the cafeteria door right beside them. It was so loud!

"Up against the wall," Marigold cried, flattening herself against the baseboard to escape being trampled.

"Everyone's so huge," yelled Nory.

Marigold was surprised by how dirty everything looked. A gum wrapper on the ground. A splooch of mud from someone's shoe. A crumpled piece of lost homework. There was junk all over the floor. She had never noticed it when she was big.

The second bell rang and the hallway emptied

with a slamming of locker doors. Lacey was gone. The tiny fifth graders were alone. They regarded one another with big eyes and huge grins.

"Hey, watch this," Nory said. She made a funny expression and fluxed into a dritten. A teeny-tiny dritten, not much bigger than a moth.

"Nice," said Marigold. She was proud of how her big magic made everyone tiny. Nory had stayed tiny even when she fluxed. Wowzers.

"We still have to go to class," Willa pointed out. She looked down the long, long hall, which looked like a highway. "Yikes, our classroom is far away."

Nory popped back from dritten to her tiny-girl form. "We should have asked Lacey to take us."

Marigold felt a wave of worry. Was this plan going to work out? Was everyone going to be miserable?

Nory, as usual, took action. "Oh, well. We're tough. Come on, team. Off we go."

Marigold felt her spirits lift.

They set off down the hall.

They walked.

And walked.

After what felt like ages, they were a third of the way to the UDM classroom. Then: *THUMP, THUMP, THUMP.*

The ground shook.

"An elephant is coming," Willa said.

"There are no elephants in school," Sebastian said.

"It could be a fluxed student," said Willa.

Marigold shivered. "Even if this isn't an elephant, there are a lot of scary animals here that I didn't think to worry about! What if a flamingo escapes from the Fuzzy lab? It would totally eat us up like shrimp."

"There are flamingos in the Fuzzy lab?" Elliott asked. The Fuzzy lab was a home to many animals used in teaching Fuzzies to use their animal-taming magic.

"Oh, yeah," said Nory. "They have a baby alligator, too." She was the only one of them who had visited the lab.

"That is not good news," said Sebastian.

"I can scare it away," said Pepper. "At least, I think I can. If my magic works the same way when I'm small."

Thump. Thump. THUMP!

"It's just Coach," Elliott said, turning to look behind them.

Coach paused as he reached the tiny kids. He scratched his head.

"We're shrunken fifth graders," Marigold said, waving. The others joined in, calling out things like "We're tiny! See?" and "Aren't we adorable?" and "Don't squish us."

Coach put his enormous meaty hands on his enormous meaty knees and squatted, peering at them. He let out a low whistle. "Hi, Nory. Kids."

"We're protesting," Marigold explained, looking back and forth between his enormous shiny eyes.

"Yeah," Nory chimed in. "We object to being told how we can play during our free time at school. We think the Dreggs ban is unfair and the principal didn't think it through. And until we're allowed to bring them to school, or at least to recess, we stay small!"

"Yeah!" chorused the others. "We made ourselves

tiny and we demand big change!" That was their slogan.

"Bax isn't with you, is he?" Coach looked worried.

"No, Coach," said Nory. "He thought it was a bad idea."

"Phew," said Coach.

"We need to get to class," Marigold told him. She glanced at the others. "If we don't go to class, the teachers won't know we're small. Plus, you know, we need an education."

"All right," Coach said. "Hey, shall I flux into a cat to carry you? I can do Persian, Abyssinian, Manx. You know, I do nineteen different house cats. You could ride on my back."

"Don't!" cried Pepper. "I'm here, remember? I'm not sure how well I can pause my fiercing magic if you flux. I paused it while Nory was Tiny-Dritten-Nory so I didn't scare her—but that was only for about thirty seconds. I don't know how being tiny will affect my magic. My magic might be tiny, too. I might not be able to pause very long and then Cat-Coach will get frightened. It could be dangerous."

Coach sighed. As everyone knew, he loved cat fluxing. "You're right. In that case, climb aboard my arm." He squatted and laid his forearm on the floor.

Marigold climbed on first. She sat facing forward, clutching the fabric of Coach's long-sleeved shirt in each hand. She felt a little wobbly—and more than a little scared.

"Don't be shy," Coach said to the rest of them.

They followed Marigold's example and took their seats on Coach's forearm.

"Standing up now," he said when they were all settled.

"Whoa!" everyone squealed, tilting and working hard to stay aboard.

"It's like a roller coaster!" Nory cried.

Marigold grinned. It wasn't scary after all. It was fun. The floor seemed miles away, and every step Coach took rumbled his arm.

Coach dropped Clyde at his Flicker class and Zinnia at her Flare class. He didn't go in and speak to either of their teachers.

Outside Ms. Starr's classroom, he stopped and frowned. "I don't think Ms. Starr is going to be pleased about this."

"That's okay," said Nory. "We are *happy* to be sent to the principal's office."

"We want to tell him why we think it's unfair," added Marigold. She felt a little nervous. After all, this whole protesting thing was new to her. But she was excited, too, and her excitement was stronger than her worry.

"If you say so," Coach said. He rapped on the classroom door, then lowered his arm to the floor. Marigold and the remaining tinies tumbled off. Everyone was flushed and excited.

I did this, Marigold thought with wonder.

14

Even with six tiny students in class, Ms. Starr acted like nothing was unusual, which Nory found extremely disappointing. Bax and Andres must have already filled her in. Ms. Starr said good morning to all the kids and lifted the tiny students onto her desk. Then she took roll and made morning announcements, just like she always did.

After a minute, Marigold and Pepper sat cross-legged on Ms. Starr's desk. Willa perched on a box of paper clips. Sebastian settled on a paperweight and Elliott on a stapler. When Nory decided to join him, their combined weight made the stapler eject a staple. *Cu-thunk!*

Ms. Starr gave them side-eye. "Nory and Elliott, please stop playing with my office supplies."

"We weren't," said Nory. "I just—"

"Kids. All of you," said Ms. Starr, setting aside her morning announcements. "I do love seeing that Marigold is feeling so confident with her magic. Marigold, I'm very proud of you. But we all know Lacey Clench went to the hospital when she shrank. So let's talk. I'm concerned this protest is dangerous."

"It's not," said Marigold. "I can make everyone big again. Didn't Layla tell you what happened in our tutoring sessions?"

"No, actually. Ms. Lapczynski has not sent me a single report," said Ms. Starr. "I've been meaning to speak to her about that."

"Well, I can big things up now," said Marigold. "I've been practicing."

"You can?" Ms. Starr looked genuinely thrilled, the way she always was when her students made progress. "Oh, Marigold, I'm so happy." Then her serious teacher face came back. "But I'm still not pleased about this protest. Andres and Bax explained it to me before you all arrived, and I really do have doubts."

Nory was frustrated. "But, Ms. Starr, our requests are reasonable. And not a single teacher or administrator has asked us kids what *we* think. Not once."

Ms. Starr pursed her lips. She sat down and rested her chin on her forearms so that she was gazing straight at the tinies. "I understand you want your toys back."

"Please don't call them toys. We prefer you call them Dreggs," Marigold said. She spoke with a confidence that surprised Nory. She marched across Ms. Starr's desk and pointed at Ms. Starr's coffee cup. "You get to bring stuff to class that doesn't have anything to do with lessons. Coffee drinks. Your phone. Even Carrot, your rabbit. Why can't we?"

Ms. Starr sighed. "Carrot isn't disruptive. The Dreggs are very disruptive."

Marigold went on. "The Dreggs ban includes lunch and recess. And the time before and after school. The principal is dictating how we play and what's in our bags. We don't think that's right."

"Well, I do respect your right to protest in a peaceful way," said Ms. Starr. "And I admit that you made a very original choice." She stood up and went to the art cupboard. "Be tiny if you want," she continued, "for today, at least. But don't expect me to make special allowances for you."

"That's fine," Nory told her. "We can take care of ourselves."

"Bax?" said Ms. Starr. "Help me spread out the art paper, please. Andres, put on your brickpack so you can work down here on the floor. Our upside-down magic lesson today will be foot painting. Remember, this exercise helps you manage new sensory input and tap into your creativity at the same time. That helps you manage your magic."

Foot painting was one of Nory's favorite activities.

"We all know art and magic are connected," said Ms. Starr. "And magic is grounded in the feet. So really stay alive to the sensations from your heels to the tips of your toes."

"Foot painting," Willa exclaimed. "We get to leave our tiny footprints!"

Ms. Starr and Bax unspooled a swath of paper across the floor. Then Ms. Starr anchored it with masking tape. She tossed the tape to Andres, who did the same.

Since there didn't seem to be any protesting to do at the moment, Nory decided to focus on the lesson. It would be amazing to foot-paint as a tiny. And at least Ms. Starr was letting them stay small.

Bax lifted the tinies down and set them on the paper. "I don't know about this whole plan, you guys," he said. "You could get yourselves squished."

"You don't need to like it. Thanks for the lift," Nory said sweetly. She skipped over to an open jar of blue paint. This was going to be fun!

"Give me a boost?" she asked Elliott.

"Sure," he said, coming over and forming a stirrup with his hands.

While Ms. Starr was rummaging in the supply cupboard for brushes and other paint colors, Nory climbed to the edge of the jar. She could just balance. The paint below glistened like a perfect lake on a perfect summer day.

She pulled off her sneakers and socks, tossed them to the ground, and rolled up the legs of her jeans. Then she carefully dipped her toes into the paint. Ooh, it felt good. She submerged her entire foot and squealed at its velvety gloopiness.

"Come on up," she called, extending a hand to Elliott.

"I'm not sure this is smart," Andres said, looming.

"It is," Nory reassured him.

"You could fall in," he said.

"You're just jealous."

Andres sighed and joined back at the other end of the huge expanse of paper. A few feet away, Marigold and Willa each held a brush. They were painting each other's feet with yellow and pink paint. Pepper stepped in and out of a small puddle of black. She made a careful, cute trail of tiny footprints across the stretch of paper. This was the usual type of thing the students did when they foot-painted. But Sebastian was making green snow angels—paint angels—nearby, laughing as he swished his arms and legs in wide arcs.

"This is awesome!" he cried.

Ms. Starr looked over at him.

Nory froze, hoping her teacher wouldn't notice her sitting on the edge of the paint can.

"Sebastian," said Ms. Starr. "Please remember that magic is grounded in the feet. This exercise is about connecting your creativity to your feet, specifically."

Ms. Starr dug her head back into the cupboard.

Sebastian stood up guiltily. He dipped his feet in a small dish of green paint and began jumping up and down, making tiny marks on the paper. Farther away, Bax foot-painted in gray and Andres in red.

Nory grinned at Elliott, who sat on the rim of the blue can with her. "I'm jumping in," she whispered. "Do you dare me?"

"Do not jump into the paint can," called Andres from where he sat, painting red onto his heels. "Just dip your feet and get on the paper, Nory!"

"Paint could be poisonous if it gets in your mouth," Elliott said.

Nory splashed headfirst into the paint, then popped to the surface. It felt wonderful and slimy.

But it did taste awful.

She treaded paint for a bit.

Why wasn't Elliott jumping in?

And . . . hmm. How was she going to get out?

And what if the paint was really poisonous?

A large hand reached down and lifted her up. "Bax!" Nory said.

"You stupid-head," he said, setting her down. He looked pale, with beads of sweat popping out on his forehead. "I can't believe you did that. Isn't foot painting wacky enough for you without swimming? You're stressing me out. I am not good with stress. You know that."

Nory saw Bax shimmer, as if he was going in and out of focus.

"Oh, no, he's about to flux," she cried. She started running, her blue footsteps tracking down the paper. "Clear the way! Bax is fluxing!"

Boom! Nory's brains shook and her bones rattled.

Now Rock-Bax loomed above her, gray and craggy. If he had crashed down even an inch closer, she'd have been a goner. Her heart hammered in her chest.

At the sound of Nory shouting, Ms. Starr stopped rummaging and turned around. Now she stood over the tinies. "Enough!" she exclaimed. "Students, please give me your attention."

Willa made a tiny *eep* of fear.

"Nory, did you swim in the paint jar?"

There was no lying about it. Nory nodded.

"Oh, dear," said Ms. Starr. "Rinse your mouth out right now." The teacher set a Dixie cup with just a little clean water in it next to Nory, plus another empty one. "Rinse! Spit into the empty cup. Rinse again. Spit." Nory could lift the Dixie cup, but drinking from it was hard. It was enormous. The water spilled down her front. But she kept rinsing and spitting.

Ms. Starr continued. "Nory and Sebastian, you have foot-painted numerous times without covering your entire bodies in paint. It's disruptive and dangerous, what you did today. It prevents your fellow students from learning, too. Here's Bax, fluxed in the middle of a lesson. Now I have to take him to the nurse." She shook her head angrily and fetched the wheelbarrow that they used to haul Rock-Bax around. At the nurse's office, he would be turned back into a boy.

Andres helped Ms. Starr lift Rock-Bax in. Ms. Starr swept her arm at the room. "Foot painting is over. Please clean this mess up. Yes, tiny students. Clean. I am really disappointed in some of you." She gripped the wheelbarrow's handles and headed into the hall, pulling the door shut behind her.

The kids looked at each other, then got to it. Andres found the plastic container of Handi-Wipes and held a wipe out to Nory. She stretched it out on the floor and rolled in it like a burrito. She hated that Ms. Starr was mad at her, but the rolling lifted her spirits. Really, wouldn't anyone be happy while rolling around in a giant Handi-Wipe?

She took a second wipe and cleaned herself off some more. Good enough. She was mostly clean, although still blue in a number of places.

Sebastian scrubbed up, too. He was definitely still green, though, especially his hair. At least his clothes weren't dripping. The others got their feet clean and put on their shoes and socks. Some of them put lids on paint jars. Others stuffed the brushes into jugs of water. Andres moved the jars back into the art cupboard and set the jugs on Ms. Starr's desk. He lifted the tape off the painted paper, picked it up, and re-taped it to the wall to dry.

Their tiny footprints and Sebastian's tiny green

angels looked amazing. Nory knew she was going to love seeing them again tomorrow, when everyone was big again.

Ooh, where was her Dregg? It was somewhere in the classroom, Nory knew. Glowie would be lonely. Maybe with Ms. Starr out of the room, Nory could pay her a visit. Maybe even rescue her!

While the rest of the students finished cleaning up, Nory crawled under the teacher's desk. Ms. Starr had left the bottom drawer open just a sliver, but it was enough. Nory dug her hands into the crack from below and walked backward in order to pull the drawer all the way open. Then she scrambled up onto the rim.

Glowie! She was right there, still in her egg. "Oh, my Dregg, I love you." Nory climbed into the drawer and hugged Glowie. Squeezed the egg. She had missed her Luminous Dragonette sooooo much.

The Dregg began to rock. And jiggle.

It was as big as Nory was.

It was a little scary, the way it was jiggling.

Pb-b-b-b-b-b-b. The Dregg's fart was so loud that Nory stumbled backward into a pile of sticky notes.

Glowie's shell cracked and opened. A massive dragon head nosed its way out. Then a massive foot with deadly-looking claws.

"Andres!" Nory shrieked. She scrambled up. "Save me! Glowie is attacking!"

Andres rushed around to the back of Ms. Starr's desk. He snatched Tiny Nory up, *zwip!* out of the drawer. Then he shucked off his brickpack and floated up to the ceiling. Nory clutched on to his thumb and laughed with relief.

"We're flying!" she cried. "Why did you fly?"

"Uh, it seemed like the right thing to do at the time," Andres said.

"It was!" said Nory. "Glowie got really scary!"

The door to the classroom opened. In strode Ms. Starr. Her eyes went first to the waddling, squawking Dregg making noise in her desk drawer. Then she looked up at Andres, who was floating with his back against the ceiling, holding Nory in one hand.

"Excuse me. Students are not to go in my drawers. Or any teacher's drawers. Ever," said Ms. Starr, her hands on her hips. "Even if I have confiscated a toy. Even if you think you have a very good reason. Do you understand? Never."

"We understand," said most everyone.

"Nory?" asked Ms. Starr, looking up.

"I understand," said Nory. Her face felt hot with shame. Father would be shocked to know one of his children had rummaged in a teacher's drawer.

"Andres, please bring Nory down," Ms. Starr requested.

Andres pushed off the ceiling and caught on to a desk with one hand, still holding Nory in the other. He set Nory on the desk and went back to the ceiling.

"We do not fly our friends, even if we can take passengers," Ms. Starr reminded Andres. "Not until we have had proper lessons. And we do not ride our friends," she said, looking at Tiny Nory. "You know that. We do not ride fluxed students and we do not ride Flyers. It doesn't matter what size you are. All of that takes education before it can be done safely." She stood with her arms folded. "I'm upset that all this happened."

Nory hung her head. "I'm sorry, Ms. Starr."

15

After magic, they did math. Then science and literature. The tiny students figured out how to break off bits of lead to use as pencils and how to jump from key to key on their calculators with their tiny bodies. Marigold broke off a piece of a thick pink eraser to use, though it was still as big as her hand. When the bell rang for lunch, she was exhausted (so much jumping!) but happy. It was time to show the rest of the fifth grade what they were up to, and how cool it was.

Bax came back from the nurse and offered to

carry the tiny students to the cafeteria in a cardboard box. Everyone climbed in. Bax held the box under one arm and Andres's leash in his other hand.

Marigold loved the feeling of going down the hall. Several people stopped Bax to see what was in the box, and Bax told them about the protest. "We made ourselves tiny, and we demand big change!" shouted Marigold. Other kids repeated the slogan and passed it on, spreading the word about her shrinking magic.

"Wow, I never saw magic like that," one kid said.

"How brave are they?" said another. "I'd never have the guts to do that, even though I want Dreggs at school, just like anyone."

"I hope they get the principal to change his stupid rule," loads of kids said.

In the cafeteria, Bax got the tiny kids two cheeseburgers to share. Marigold and her friends sat around the burgers, picking up handfuls of warm, cheesy meat and shoving them into their mouths.

It was amazing, sharing a giant community

cheeseburger. Marigold's hands got covered in grease. It dripped down her chin, too.

When she was done eating, she looked to see dozens of kids gathered around. All those faces seemed huge.

"That's Elliott who lives on my block," one kid said, pointing. "Hi, Elliott."

"He's sliding on a pickle!" said another kid. "He's using it as a sled."

"Sure am," cried Tiny Elliott cheerfully. He and Sebastian had used an upside-down lunch tray and a napkin dispenser to make a hill. He climbed to the top of the hill with the pickle held in front of him, then jumped onto it, sitting cross-legged as it spun down the lunch tray slide. "Yahoo! Yeah!"

"Zamboozle, I want to ride a pickle," said a fifth-grade Flicker named Fabienne. "Who's the one with the wonky shrinking magic?" Her enormous eyes landed on Marigold. "Are you the boss? Can you shrink me, please?"

"It's not kind to say wonky," said Marigold politely.

"We prefer *different* or *unusual*. But yes, I'd be *happy* to shrink you. We are protesting the ban on Dreggs. The more tiny students, the better."

For a split second, she worried that being small would affect her magic. But she closed her eyes and focused . . . and it worked. Fabienne shrank! Marigold's size didn't mess up her magic at all.

"Shrink me, too!" said Fabienne's friend Blaze.

"Me too, me too!" came a chorus of voices.

Marigold waved her tiny arms and climbed onto a juice box that had fallen over. "All fifth graders who want your Dregg privileges restored, say aye!"

"Aye!" cried dozens of fifth graders, and the cafeteria shook with the force of their combined voices.

"And if you're willing to turn *tiny* in order to effect a *massive* change, say aye!" called Marigold.

"Aye!" Kids thumped the table and stomped the floor.

"This is awesome," Nory yelled.

"I know," Marigold yelled back. The two girls grinned.

Marigold raised her hands, signaling for attention. She looked from giant face to giant face the way she'd seen countless teachers do, waiting for every last kid to hush.

"If you want to be shrunk in order to protest the ban on Dreggs, please line up," Marigold instructed. "Once you've shrunk, Bax will put you on the table. Big people, be careful not to step on your classmates. Understood?"

"Understood!" chorused the new recruits. People pushed and wiggled as they got into line. The protest was growing. At least two dozen kids lined up to be shrunk. Even Lacey Clench got in line.

"Hold up!" exclaimed one of the fifth-grade Flickers. It was Rainey, Clyde's friend. "Marigold, tell them to let me through!"

Marigold nodded, and the kids separated to give Rainey room. Rainey walked over and opened up their hands, and out spilled Tiny Clyde and Tiny Zinnia.

"Clyde will lead the tiny Flickers under my

supervision," cried Marigold, pointing to Clyde. "And Zinnia will lead the tiny Flares!"

The kids stomped the floor and cheered.

"Fluxers, Fuzzies, and Flyers, I'll choose leaders once you're shrunk," continued Marigold. She spent the remainder of the lunch period shrinking new recruits, all of whom Bax helpfully, but grouchily, deposited onto the tabletop.

By the time Marigold was done, the tinies had grown in number from eight to thirty-eight.

"Not bad," Sebastian said with a whistle.

"Are you kidding?" said Nory. "Marigold, we are rock stars." Her eyes shone with awe.

"Elinor Horace and Marigold Ramos?" There was a lunch teacher looming over them.

Uh-oh.

"The two of you are summoned to the principal's office immediately," said the lunch teacher. "And I'm taking you in this piece of Tupperware."

16

Bouncing along with Marigold in the Tupperware, Nory was nervous. Yes, she had said she'd be happy to get sent to the principal, and she *did* want to make the demands of the protest clear. But now that it was happening, as the daughter of a headmaster, she was filled with dread. Father would not be supportive of this protest, she realized. Not at all. Would Principal Gonzalez?

They reached the office, but there was no one in the room. The lunch teacher deposited them on the desk and left.

"Ah," said the principal. "My tiny protest leaders."

He shimmered into view. The principal was a very powerful Flicker. He often walked the halls invisibly, checking up on students. He might even have seen them in the cafeteria, Nory realized.

Visible, Principal Gonzalez was a tall man, with no hair on his head and a big mustache. He wore a suit and a bow tie.

He took a seat at the desk and leaned forward. His gaze was serious as he looked first at Nory, then at Marigold.

"We have a problem," he said.

Eep. It was hard enough being brave in front of the principal when you were your usual size. It was even harder when you were only three inches high. Nory felt herself start to sweat. Then her vision went blurry.

Uh-oh.

Pop!

She was Tiny-Koat-Nory. She had fluxed by accident into a kitten-goat. She had a kitten head and body, goat legs, the most adorable little horns, and a tendency to eat everything in sight. It was usually a fun shape to be, but Koat-Nory did have trouble keeping her human mind. Now she was about one inch high.

"Ooh, look at the mini—what is it?" asked Principal Gonzalez.

Marigold sighed and sounded annoyed. "She's a koat. Nory, flux back. We're talking to the principal."

"Did she flux by accident?" asked the principal. "She does that, I know. But we haven't had any big incidents since the start of the school year."

Tiny-Koat-Nory leapt and cavorted over the items on the principal's desk, like an obstacle course. She could hear them talking about her, but she didn't really care. Goats loved to leap and climb, and so did kittens!

Leap! She cleared the stapler.

Leap! She cleared the label maker.

Up, up, up! She climbed the stack of books and sat on the top. "Baaaaa!!"

"Nory!" shouted Marigold.

Tiny-Koat-Nory found the edge of a book jacket and had started to chew. Nom nom nom!

"Do not chew Principal Gonzalez's copy of *Happy Children, Orderly Schools*!" yelled Marigold. "We are trying to have a protest negotiation, and you are ruining it!"

Nom nom nom, delicious book jacket.

Oh, what?

Enormous fingers gently picked up Tiny-Koat-Nory and placed her back on the desktop, next to that yelling girl. Tiny-Koat-Nory was disappointed, but she looked on the bright side. The yelling girl was wearing a delicious-looking fuzzy sweater. And now Tiny-Koat-Nory could have a bite.

"Ahhhh!" yelled Marigold, batting at Tiny-Koat-Nory's nose. "Nory, I'm serious. Flux back right now. You are off topic. We're here to fight for having Dreggs at school again."

Deep inside Tiny-Koat-Nory, Girl-Nory heard the message. *Zwingo*, she thought. *I better try and flux back.*

Pop pop pop! She was Tiny Nory again, standing next to Marigold with a mouth full of angora. She spit it out into her hand and shoved the fluff into her pocket, hoping the principal hadn't noticed. "Sorry about your sweater," she whispered to Marigold.

"We need to be a united front," whispered Marigold. She swallowed hard. "This is our chance to make the protest work!"

"Please forgive me, Principal Gonzalez," said Nory, using her talking-to-grown-ups voice. "Marigold and I are glad you called us to speak with you."

Principal Gonzalez looked grave. "I really am concerned here. I walked invisibly into the cafeteria at lunch to find you'd shrunk a considerable portion of the fifth grade."

"Thirty-eight tiny students, sir," said Nory.

"I can grow them back," said Marigold. "Don't worry about that."

"And why are you shrinking them?" asked the principal.

"We're demanding big change!" cried Marigold.

Then in a quieter voice, she said, "We respectfully protest the banning of Dreggs. We do not think it's fair for you to decide how we play and what we play with during free time at school. And you did not listen to student voices before you banned them. You never heard our perspective. So . . . yeah. We caused a peaceful disruption."

"Parents will not be pleased if their kids come home tiny," he said. "I have experience with kids going home invisible. People—especially parents, but sometimes kids as well—get really upset."

"I can un-shrink them at the end of the day," Marigold said. "Every kid who's a tiny *chose* to be a tiny. They *chose* to be part of the protest because they want to bring the Dreggs to school."

"The Dreggs cause trouble," said the principal. "The teachers can't teach with them hatching and hopping in the classroom."

"But they're bringing kids together," explained Nory. "And Dreggs are especially good for the kids in the Upside-Down Magic class."

"How so?" asked Mr. Gonzalez.

"Other kids make fun of us," said Marigold. "I know you told them not to, but they still do. They call us wonkos, or they steer clear of us in the halls, like they're scared to be near us."

Ooh! Marigold made a good point. "But since we introduced Dreggs to the school, kids started liking us," Nory added. "We went to a party at Clyde's house, and there were Flickers and Fluxers there. Two Flares are helping with our protest. And just now, in the lunchroom, I know we shrank some Fuzzies and Flyers. That means kids from all five Fs care enough about Dreggs to stop being nervous around kids with upside-down magic. That's good for us, and it's good for them. Don't you think?"

Principal Gonzalez tapped his lower lip. "Hmm," he said. "I hadn't thought of it that way."

"Thank you, sir," said Nory in her politest voice.

"Tell you what," he said. "How about I let the fifth graders bring Dreggs to school every Friday, to be taken out only during recess? Never in the classroom, never in the cafeteria—but A-OK in the yard on Fridays?"

Nory glowed. "Yes, sir, that would be great. Thank you." She had won. Or rather, she and Marigold had made their point and convinced the principal!

Marigold cleared her throat. "I'm sorry, but no," she said.

Nory swiveled her head. "Marigold, this is a really good compromise," she whispered.

"It's not good enough." Marigold blinked anxiously, but stood her ground. "I learned from my tutor that sometimes, protests need time to build. People are nervous at first. But today we got thirty new people on board. More could join tomorrow! Principal Gonzalez, we do appreciate your offer. But we can't accept."

"Fridays is my best compromise," said Mr. Gonzalez. "I'm not going to make another."

"Fridays are good," said Nory. "We do accept! We one hundred percent do!"

"I'm sorry. We do not," repeated Marigold. She

was clenching and unclenching her fists, Nory noticed. "Until you allow Dreggs at school every day, at least for recess and when we're not in class, I'll keep shrinking anyone who asks me to. Even if Nory backs down, I'm keeping this protest going."

17

The office secretary called Ms. Starr to send a student to collect Nory and Marigold. The two girls waited in the hall outside the principal's office, on a hard bench.

The moment they were alone, Nory blew up. Marigold was expecting it.

"Why did you ruin everything?" barked Nory. "Principal Gonzalez met us halfway!"

"It wasn't halfway. He said we could have Dreggs one-eighth of the day, only one time a week. That means he met us one-fortieth of the way," explained Marigold.

"He offered a compromise, Marigold! A *compromise*!"

"Yes," Marigold said. "But the compromise was bad. And we are just getting started. Don't you see?"

"It was a good compromise," Nory insisted. "We *won*."

Bax arrived, holding the cardboard box. Nory and Marigold climbed in, still arguing. As they stepped around the corner, a Flare named Rune came down the hall with five tiny Flares sitting in his hand.

"There they are," one tiny Flare cried. "With the grumpy boy!"

"Speed up, Rune!" said Tiny Lacey. "I want to hear the news."

Marigold felt a surge of energy. She would tell the Flares about the way they'd stood up to the principal. She'd offer to shrink Rune and the rest of the Flares, to make the Big Shrink even bigger!

A group of fifth-grade Flickers swarmed up as

well, holding a gerbil cage full of tiny Flickers. They were eager for answers, too.

"So? Do we get to bring our Dreggs back?" Clyde asked. "What happened?"

"We won, but Marigold ruined it," Nory said.

"No. We stood our ground," said Marigold. "Principal Gonzalez offered a very weak compromise. Fridays at recess only. But more and more kids are joining our protest. We don't have to have Dreggs only on Fridays. If we stick with it, we can have them every day of the week."

"Marigold told him she'd keep shrinking people," explained Nory. "She threatened the principal."

"I did not threaten him. I said our protest was growing and I would keep shrinking kids who wanted it. It's a peaceful protest, like we learn about in social studies," shouted Marigold. "Do we give in?" she called to the crowd.

"No!" called some of the kids.

"We do not give in!" Marigold proclaimed. "We can get him to give us a better offer. We just need more fifth graders to turn tiny. Who's in?"

Rune didn't volunteer, but almost all the Flickers raised their hands. So did several nearby Flyers. Marigold concentrated, sent the magic through her fingers, and *zwoop, zwoop, zwoop!* The Flyers shrank.

"They're so cute!" somebody said.

The tiny Flyers zipped in between people's legs, none of them more than a foot in the air.

Next, Marigold instructed the big Flickers to put down the gerbil cage. Once they were all tiny, everyone piled into the cage. Rune, who had stayed large, would carry it.

"Excuse me," said Tiny Lacey, banging on the door to the gerbil cage. "Marigold? I want to change back. Never mind about the protest."

"What?" Marigold was shocked.

"Well, my magic is small now that I'm small," said Lacey. "I really don't like it, and later today we're doing cooking projects in magic class. I want my fire back."

"Yeah, me too," chorused the tiny Flares. They

started complaining about how small their magic had gotten. They could only make tiny sparks.

Hmm. Marigold thought about what they were saying. True, some of the kids' magic had gotten small when they got small. But Marigold was still able to shrink things. And Nory was still able to flux just fine—just not into anything large. How did it all work? There was still so much about magic they didn't understand.

In any case, the tiny Flares shouldn't grow large now. "You'll ruin the protest if you big up," Marigold said. "You have to wait until the end of the school day at least."

Lacey's mouth fell open. "I don't think you heard me. I need my full-sized fire back."

"I did hear you," Marigold said. "And I said no."

"I *said* change me back."

"No. We're in the middle of a protest."

The other tiny Flares shouted that they wanted to be big again, too.

Marigold refused. "We have to stay strong," she

urged. "Don't you guys get it? If we all turn tiny, Principal Gonzalez will have to meet our demands."

"But, Marigold, why do you get to decide?" a tiny Flare asked. "If it's a group protest, shouldn't it be a group decision?"

"I'm okay with the protest ending," said another tiny Flare. "I want it to end!"

Marigold shook her head. "I'm doing this for all of us. For the whole school. You'll thank me. You'll see."

The bell rang to end recess. People scattered. "I'll get you for this, Marigold!" cried Lacey Clench, shaking her tiny fist as Rune walked down the hall, carrying her and the others in the gerbil cage. The tiny Flyers swarmed off to class. Nory, Bax, and Marigold stood alone in the hall.

Nory glared at Marigold. "If people want to be changed back, you have to change them back!" she said.

Marigold pressed her lips together. She twined her foot around her ankle.

"You think it's fair to force them to do the protest?" Nory asked.

"They committed to doing it! They shouldn't back out in the middle."

"Seriously?" said Nory.

"Yes! Seriously!" Seeing a protest through to the end *was* serious. Why didn't Nory understand?

A shadow loomed over them.

"The two of you are driving me batty," Bax growled from above. "You're stressing me out and I don't want to flux, so . . ." He folded in the flaps of the cardboard box, making a lid. Everything went dark. He'd closed them in! "We're going back to class," he said as he strode down the hall. "And we're not going to talk about the protest anymore. We're going to be quiet, and then we're going to listen to Ms. Starr explain our volcano research projects."

"But why?" Marigold said, calling through the crack of light that shone between the flaps.

"Because I say so," Bax said. "And guess what? I'm bigger than you, so what I say goes."

18

Back in class, Nory sulked. The Big Shrink was out of control. Marigold was being unreasonable. If they didn't big up the kids who wanted to go back to normal, all the good feelings between the UDM kids and the typical kids would disappear. But what could she do?

Nothing, that's what. Marigold had the power.

Nory wanted to tell Pepper all about it. And Elliott. But she couldn't even do that, because as soon as Bax brought her and Marigold to class, Ms. Starr launched into the day's lecture on volcanoes.

She let the tiny kids sit on her desk so they could see the board. She showed them a diagram. And another video. She talked about the three different kinds of lava monsters and the way they only appeared during volcano eruptions.

While a third video ran and Ms. Starr stepped out to use the restroom, a terrifying creature leapt out of Ms. Starr's top drawer and bounded across the desk toward the kids.

"Ahhhhh!" Nory screamed.

The creature was mammoth, with frighteningly fluffy fur and enormous ears. There was no tail that Nory could see from this angle. Huge, dangerous front teeth and gigantic, bizarrely long whiskers. It hopped over to her, weird whiskers trembling.

Pop! Nory fluxed into Tiny-Dritten-Nory, in order to fight it with her fire breath.

Pffff! She spurted fire breath at it, but the creature paid no attention. The fire breath was really tiny, after all. Nory's dritten was only a half an inch high.

Tiny-Dritten-Nory flapped into the air and hissed

at the monster. She dive-bombed it, but it swatted her away with one enormous paw.

Maybe Pepper would fierce it, thought Tiny-Dritten-Nory. Maybe Elliott would freeze it. Even though he was never supposed to use his freezing magic on living creatures, this was an emergency!

There was a lot of screaming.

Tiny-Dritten-Nory saw Tiny Elliott bravely try to zap the creature with ice, but his magic, like his body, had turned small. A sheen of frost appeared on the creature's fur, but nothing more. Now the creature was bending over Pepper, wiggling its terrible snout. Pepper's magic was doing nothing.

Sebastian had grabbed a pencil and was approaching the monster as if to poke it in the backside, but the creature was on the move. It sniffed and poked its terrifying toothy face at the kids, who scrambled across the desk in all directions. Tiny-Dritten-Nory hovered above, her mind racing. Andres was on the ceiling. Where was Bax? When would Ms. Starr be back from the restroom?

What could Nory do to save her friends?

Bax's hand came down from the sky. He began to—what?! Was he petting the creature? What was wrong with that boy?

Thank goodness Marigold stepped bravely in front of the monster and magicked it.

Zwoop!

The creature shrank.

Zwoop!

Bax shrank, too.

Omigosh.

Well.

It looked really different, now that it was tiny. The creature was Carrot, Ms. Starr's companion bunny. Not a monster at all.

And omigosh again. Tiny Bax was on the floor.

Pop! Tiny-Dritten-Nory fluxed back to her tiny-girl self. They all rushed to the edge of the desk, peering down at Tiny Bax.

"Wh-what?" cried Tiny Bax, holding out his tiny arms and examining them. "Marigold, you shrank me!"

"I didn't mean to," Marigold cried. "I'm so sorry!"

Nory stamped her foot. All her anger at Marigold came rushing back. "You are out of control!" she told Marigold. "You're so shrink-happy, you're shrinking people willy-nilly."

"I was protecting us from the monster," Marigold argued. Then she stopped and flushed. "I shrank Bax by accident."

"The monster was only Carrot," said Nory.

"It was?" Marigold looked around.

Tiny Carrot nodded. "Sorry I scared you," the bunny said. "I slept all day. And then when I saw the six of you, so tiny and cute, I just wanted to sniff you. Rabbits use their sense of smell nearly as much as their eyes, you know. It never occurred to me that you didn't recognize me or I would have said something."

"It's okay," said Nory.

"I'm sorry I shrank you," said Marigold. "I was really scared."

"Not a problem," said Carrot. "As long as you make me big again later."

From high above, Andres complained, "Am I the only regular-sized kid left? Who's going to hold my leash on the way out of school to meet my sister? Is *Ms. Starr* going to have to hold my leash?"

Tiny Bax looked up at Andres. "I didn't ask to be shrunk, believe me. And I am really not happy about it."

"I'm sorry," Marigold said. "I've said I'm sorry a thousand times!"

"Marigold," said Nory, exasperated. "Quit saying sorry and just turn Bax back. He doesn't want to be tiny. It's a health risk."

Tiny Bax leaned forward at his waist, bracing his hands against his thighs. "You guys are stressing me out," he said. "Can everyone just back off?"

Tiny Bax quivered and shook.

"Uh-oh," Elliott said. "He looks like he's going to flux."

And sure enough, he fluxed. Tiny Bax was now a small rock.

More of a stone, really.

A pebble.

"Too late," Pepper said.

Nory stared at Pebble-Bax and clapped her hand to her mouth. If something bad happened to Bax, if Bax was permanently damaged or hurt in any way, she would never forgive herself.

"Big him up, *now*," she told Marigold shakily.

"Oh, my friends!" Ms. Starr cried, rushing back into the room. "What just happened?"

"Marigold shrank Bax and Carrot!" Nory said.

"By accident!" Marigold added.

"But Bax fluxed!" Nory cried.

"Watch out, everyone," Ms. Starr said. She rushed over and used a Dixie cup to scoop up Pebble-Bax. "Now he won't get lost or crushed." Ms. Starr gave a quick shake of her head and said, "Marigold, I'm going to have to insist that you change him back. And Carrot, too. It's not right to shrink *anyone* without permission."

Ms. Starr set Pebble-Bax's Dixie cup on the desk. Nory peeked over alongside Marigold. Pebble-Bax looked . . . like a pebble. "Change him back," said the teacher. "First Bax, then the bunny. No arguments. You wouldn't want to see Bax get hurt, would you?"

"No, never," Marigold whispered. "I would never want to hurt anyone."

"Right, then," Ms. Starr said. "Please step back to the edge of the desk so you're a safe distance. I don't want Rock-Bax to crush you once he's big again. Go ahead."

Nory, Marigold, and the rest stepped to one side of the desk. Marigold climbed up on top of a pile of books so she could see Pebble-Bax. She squinted and gestured with her hands. *Zwoop!*

Ms. Starr, looking down into the Dixie cup, inhaled sharply.

"What?" Nory demanded. She ran forward to look in. "What happened?"

Ms. Starr's skin looked damp. "Marigold, you didn't big him up. You shrank him again!" Her eyes flew over the others. "He's a speck of sand now. Bax is a speck of sand!"

19

Marigold's mind whirled.

She concentrated all of her magic on the speck of sand in the Dixie cup. She took a mental snapshot of Sand-Bax, enlarged it, and let the energy go through her forehead just as Layla had taught her—

Zwip-pfiff-ploop!

Ms. Starr blinked out of sight and then reappeared, four inches tall, just a little bigger than Marigold, Willa, and the other tiny fifth graders.

"Marigold!" cried Tiny Ms. Starr, her voice high and small. "Something is wrong. You are not bigging up. You are only shrinking. I want us all to remain calm. Let's remember our upside-down magic techniques. Do you think slow breathing would help you right now, to center your magic? Or a headstand?"

Marigold shook her head. She didn't understand what had gone wrong, but she knew no headstand was going to fix it.

"Call Layla," she said under her breath. She said it again and again, like a mantra, and with each repetition she grew more intense. Only Layla could help. She needed Layla. She clutched her head. Everything was falling apart!

Willa grabbed Marigold's hands. "Shh," she said. "We're doing what you said. We're calling Layla right now. See?"

Marigold followed Willa's gaze. She saw Andres, down from the ceiling, wearing his brickpack and digging in Ms. Starr's purse, which was on a shelf.

He found the teacher's phone. Tiny Ms. Starr barked instructions. "Now go to my contacts. Look up Layla Lapczynski. Did you find her? Yes?"

Andres pressed a button on the phone, then another. He turned the phone around, and Marigold heard an echoing ring. He'd put the call on speakerphone.

"Good job," Ms. Starr said, her voice a bit more wavery than usual. She hovered over Bax's Dixie cup and pressed the back of her hand to her forehead.

Marigold ran toward the phone. Her heart pounded, and she readied herself to yell into the speaker.

C'mon, Layla, she thought. *Pick up.*

"Hiya," blared Layla's lazy voice. "Layla here—or rather, *not* here if you've reached this message. You know what to do."

There was a long beep. Then nothing.

"Try again," Ms. Starr told Andres.

Andres tried again. But again, the voicemail.

Marigold's heart sank, but she left a message. "Layla, it's Marigold. We have an emergency at school.

This is my teacher's phone. Please call back as soon as you get this. We need your help."

Ms. Starr was speaking again, instructing Andres to fetch the nurse. When Nurse Riley arrived, he surveyed the scene and phoned the hospital.

"Yes, you heard me correctly," he said. "A mass shrinkage. Six children in human form, one rabbit, one adult, and one child who fluxed into a grain of sand. Yes, sand. And we'll need—what's that?"

Elliott, Willa, and the others talked on top of one another, hurrying to tell Nurse Riley the rest of the awful details. He listened, his expression growing increasingly alarmed, then returned to the call.

"Ah, strike that," he said into the phone. "Sounds like . . . well . . . dozens of students. Upwards of thirty, maybe quite a lot more, and yes, all tiny. Plus the rabbit and the grain of sand. What? Now? Yes, I understand. Yes, of course. See you soon."

Nurse Riley ended the call and gazed at Marigold, who burned with humiliation. *I know*, she thought. *It's all my fault.*

She slumped to the ground and put her head in her hands, knowing Ms. Starr would look after Bax and Carrot. Twenty minutes later, parents began arriving in the UDM classroom, and presumably, elsewhere at school. Nurse Riley had told everyone that Marigold was unable to big them up. The tiny kids all had to go to the hospital. Nurse Riley was taking the kids whose parents couldn't come and get them.

Nory's aunt Margo got to their class first. She took Nory and Elliott, whose dad was home with his baby brother. Then Willa's mom came. Then Pepper's mom. And Bax's dad, who was weeping as he took Sand-Bax off in the Dixie cup. Sebastian's parents came together, both of them Flyers who hovered nervously a couple of inches above the ground.

Out in the hallway, other parents walked by, holding their tiny children in cupped hands. Principal Gonzalez stood in the doorway and acted like a traffic guard, directing them to go straight to the hospital and ask for Dr. Garibaldi. "Tell her you're with the Big Shrink," he instructed.

"Utterly unacceptable," one mom said.

"I'm so scared," said a father.

"I knew it was a bad idea, bringing in these upside-down kids with their wonky magic," said a third.

Marigold wanted to die from the shame. How had she felt so proud of her powers all day, and suddenly they were back to being out of control and terrible? But that was how it was. She sat on the desk and watched Andres bring Carrot in her Dixie cup to Ms. Starr. Tiny Ms. Starr fussed over the bunny, lugging a ziplock bag of broccoli over and breaking off small pieces for Tiny Carrot to eat.

"I'll stay at school until the end of the day," said Ms. Starr to Andres. "Then Principal Gonzalez will take me and Carrot to the hospital, too. But, Andres, I think you'd better just work on your poetry essay or do some independent reading. I don't quite have the energy to go through my lesson plan, when everyone else is at the doctor."

"Sure thing, Ms. Starr," said Andres. He chose a book and began to read.

"Sweetheart?" said a kind voice. Marigold felt the rise of warm tears. It was Grandmom Flora, standing before her with Granddad Lorenzo. They'd come to pick her up.

Were they mad? Or disappointed?

"We were so worried when we got the call," said Grandmom. "Are you okay?"

Marigold began to cry. "I did this!" she wailed. "I got so wrapped up in making things better for everyone that I made things ten thousand times worse! I made everyone have to go to the *hospital*!

Grandmom Flora stroked Marigold's hair with the tip of her finger. "You're okay," she said soothingly. "It's all going to be okay."

They had brought a fuzzy mitten to carry her in. Marigold broke off a piece of a giant tissue and wiped her face. She climbed into the mitten. Grandmom held her carefully on the way to the hospital. They went by bus. It wasn't far.

"Hush now," Grandmom Flora said, since Marigold was still sniffling. "You were doing what you thought best. Fighting for student rights, yes? And, Marigold, that's admirable. When I was younger, I took part in protests, too."

"You did?" Tiny Marigold said.

"You better believe she did," said Granddad Lorenzo. "Women's rights, changes in school policies, changes in national policies. Whatever was unjust, your grandmom marched for it."

Grandmom Flora smiled. "I did. You have to stand up for what you believe in." She paused, as if picking her words carefully. "Of course, you also have to know when to back down. Backing down, sometimes, is the only way to get back on track."

Marigold's face flamed.

Grandmom Flora tucked her finger beneath Marigold's chin. "Hey now, sweetie. Don't be too hard on yourself. You're a kid. Kids are supposed to get things wrong sometimes."

"I wish I had gotten it right. Or that I could do

something—anything!—to make it right, now that it's happened!" She hated that all the tinies would have to be re-grown by having shots—ten of them!—and then have to drink multiple glasses of coconut water.

Oh. Maybe there *was* a way to make things right. Marigold sat up straighter in the mitten. She had an idea. Maybe her magic had gotten messed up because she, herself, was tiny. Which meant her *magic* was tiny. Like how Tiny Pepper could only hold back her fiercing for tiny amounts of time! And Tiny Elliott only made a little bit of frost. And the tiny Flares had only baby-sized sparks.

If Marigold regrew first—if *she* got poked by all ten needles and *she* drank the glasses and glasses of coconut water—then her magic would re-grow, too! And then—oh, zwingo! *She could big up the tinies herself, with her magic!* They wouldn't have to have all those shots. Zero needles. Zero coconut water.

True, the parents might not all let her magic their kids again, but she could offer. She could absolutely offer, couldn't she?!

• • •

Dr. Garibaldi was a tall, thin woman with slicked-back hair and wire-rimmed spectacles. She wore a white coat and spoke with a gentle Italian accent. "So you're the one responsible for all this shrinkage?" she said.

Marigold gulped. "Y-yes." At her request, Grandmom had called the hospital, stalling the other tinies from getting their shots until Marigold got there. She was the first patient to be seen.

The doctor held a stethoscope to Marigold's chest, then sighed and let it fall away. "This thing's too big to use with you tiny patients. Could you shrink the end of it? Just one end, so I can still put it in my ears?"

"I think so," Marigold answered.

The doctor took apart the stethoscope and gave Marigold the tubing and the chest piece to shrink.

Marigold concentrated, aimed, and thrust her magic at the parts of the stethoscope. They turned small with a *pop*.

"Wow," said Dr. Garibaldi. "That's remarkable." She turned the tiny pieces over in her hands and began to attach the tiny tubing back into the big ear pieces. "Do you realize what a boon you could be to the field of medicine? Once you get your magic under control?"

Marigold wasn't sure what a "boon" was, but the way Dr. Garibaldi said it made it sound good. "I could?"

"Magic like yours? Absolutely," Dr. Garibaldi said. "Think what tiny surgeons could do with tiny hands and tiny instruments. Much more delicate operations than they can do with big hands. For certain patients, it would be lifesaving. Or let's think in simpler terms. You could shrink pills for people who have trouble swallowing them."

Yeah, thought Marigold. *Maybe I could.*

The doctor chuckled. "If you can get your magic to do those kinds of things, you will make a really big difference in the world." Dr. Garibaldi held up a tray. "You're ten years old, right?" she said. "So you need ten shots."

Ugh. Ten shots.

"I can't make them small because then my fingers

won't be able to work them," continued the doctor. "After that, you'll go to the recovery room, where you'll have to drink eighteen cups of coconut water. Are you ready?"

Marigold did not like the look of those giant syringes at all. But she had no choice. She concentrated on her plan to spare the rest of the kids, or at least *maybe* spare the rest of them.

She squished her eyes shut and nodded. "I'm ready."

After Marigold felt her body expand like a piece of bubble gum becoming a bubble, she was her usual size. In the recovery room, she drank her eighteen cups of coconut water. Then she shrank a box of tissues in the examining room. Then she bigged it. Then she shrank it. And bigged it.

She was right! Her magic worked smoothly now that she wasn't shrunken. She tracked down Dr. Garibaldi and gave her the news. Together they stepped back into the waiting area.

Marigold cleared her throat. "I think I can help

everyone," she said nervously. "Is anyone willing to give me a chance to grow them? Doctor Garibaldi will stand by. Just in case."

The doctor nodded.

"No way," snapped a Flare parent. "You've done enough."

"Same here," said a Flicker parent.

The room was quiet. So many upset parents. So many tiny students. Marigold felt her heart sink.

But Nory raised her tiny hand. She stood on the armrest of her aunt's chair and said, "Instead of being poked with ten ginormous needles? Yes, please! Big me up, Marigold!"

"Me too," said Willa, from her perch on her mother's knee.

Elliott, Sebastian, and Pepper raised their hands, too. As did Rainey, Clyde, and Zinnia.

Marigold melted in relief. After everything, her friends still believed in her. "Nory, why don't I try you first? Just in case."

"Oh, gee, thanks," Nory said. Then she grinned.

"Okay, fine!" Her aunt nodded and carried her into the doctor's office.

In the examining room, Marigold closed her eyes. She took a mental snapshot of Nory, enlarged it, and let the energy go through her forehead.

Zwoop! Nory popped back to her regular size!

"You did it!" Nory cried, giving Marigold a high five. "It didn't hurt or anything!"

"Well done, Marigold," said Dr. Garibaldi. She looked Nory over, checking her pulse and temperature. "Very impressive. Nory, you don't need the shots, but I would still like you to drink the eighteen cups of coconut water in the recovery room. It's not just to help with re-growing. People can get very dehydrated with abrupt size changes."

"I'd rather not, please," Nory said. "I feel fine!"

"Nory," said Nory's aunt. "You have to do what the doctor says."

Nory rolled her eyes, but headed for the recovery room. "If you insist. Sheesh!" She stopped and looked over her shoulder. "Great job, Marigold."

20

The next day, everybody was back to their regular shapes and sizes. Even Bax.

First the doctors had used Bax's usual medicine to flux him from a grain of sand into a boy about an eighth of an inch high: Super-Tiny-Bax.

Then Marigold had bigged him back up, just like she had done with everyone else.

She was so relieved. In the end, after they saw how good Nory felt, every single student had given her a chance to big them up. Even the ones with cranky parents.

Except for Lacey Clench, that is. Her father had refused to let Marigold near his daughter.

Poor Lacey had to get the shots. All ten of them. Again.

The next morning at school felt strangely normal. Carrot was sitting on the teacher's desk, eating an apple Willa had brought her. Nory was clowning around with Elliott. Ms. Starr was getting organized to take roll and do morning announcements.

Marigold still felt awful about all the problems she'd caused. For a little while, and for the first time ever, she'd felt so powerful. And she had wanted to bring people together and help the kids have their voices heard. Only, she hadn't stopped to wonder whether she was putting people in danger, and she hadn't known how best to use her power. As a result, she had *mis*used it.

On top of that, the students hadn't even won their Dregg privileges back. In fact, the only good thing that had come out of all of the mess was Marigold's private conversation with Dr. Garibaldi.

She'd learned about how her magic could have uses in medicine, and then about the hospital's junior candy stripers program, the Peppermint Puffs.

Candy stripers were high schoolers who volunteered in the hospital to learn about medical careers. Peppermint Puffs were middle schoolers. Marigold's grandparents let Marigold sign up for Peppermint Puffs then and there.

She was, therefore, already officially a Peppermint Puff, and her first shift was next week after school. She'd don the red-and-white-striped apron that all the Peppermint Puffs wore and she'd spend the afternoon volunteering: delivering flowers, running nonmedical errands for doctors, reading stories to sick kids, and having conversations with patients who were lonely.

Marigold wouldn't get to shrink stuff as a Peppermint Puff. Not yet. But maybe she could use her shrinking magic to entertain the kids. Maybe.

From deep inside her reverie, Marigold heard someone saying her name.

"Yes?" Marigold replied.

Ms. Starr gestured to the front of the classroom, where Layla stood with her spine resting against the door frame. "Your tutor is here," Ms. Starr said.

Layla waved.

Marigold hopped up and joined her, taking her hand and dragging her into the hall. "Where were you?" she demanded. "Ms. Starr and I left an emergency message."

"Oh?" Layla said. She scratched her nose. "Now that you mention it, I guess I did see Eloise's name on my voice mail. But I didn't have time to listen to it. Was it really an emergency?"

"Yes. We had a big problem," said Marigold. "I needed you to re-grow us. My bigging-up magic wouldn't work and there were all these kids who were stuck being tiny."

"Sorry," said Layla. "I would have helped if I'd known, but I ignore my phone a lot. I have a ton of research and writing to do."

Marigold exhaled a big rush of air. What was

there to say? She had to face it: Layla would never be the tutor of her dreams.

In fact, Layla was pretty self-involved.

To be fair, Layla did know how to big things up, and she *had* taught Marigold how to do it. But strangely enough, the biggest thing Layla taught Marigold was that magic was about more than technique. Magic had to be used responsibly, and Layla . . . well, Layla was kind of irresponsible.

"I tried to un-shrink people but I made them smaller instead," she told Layla at last. "They wouldn't big up. It was because I was tiny. I had to go to the hospital to get big and then I was able to re-grow them."

"So you figured it out on your own. Good job." Layla patted Marigold on the back. "I'd like to know why people's magic got small when their bodies were small, though. That's an interesting development. Still, we can't really talk now. I'm actually only here to say that I can't meet today. The boyfriend and I are going on a road trip to the Shakespeare festival in Owl City."

"Oh," Marigold said. "All right, then."

"But I'll give it some thought and get back to you. Okay, M-Boogie?"

"Okay."

"Ciao-ciao!" Layla called as she loped down the hall and disappeared from sight.

Marigold watched her go. That Layla.

After lunch, Principal Gonzalez rapped on the door of the Upside-Down Magic classroom. He was fully visible. Everyone perked up.

"I'd like to speak to Marigold and Nory, please."

Marigold and Nory shot out of their chairs and followed him down the hall.

"How are you both feeling today?" he asked.

"Fine," Nory said. "No lasting damage."

He laughed. Marigold felt her cheeks heat up. She knew she had to be in trouble. Kids had gone to the hospital because of her. Even if everyone was okay now.

Principal Gonzalez waved hello to his assistant and motioned for the two girls to sit down. "As I'm sure you're aware, yesterday's protest caused a lot of issues," he said. "People were scared their kids would be stuck tiny. Parents were upset. My administration was upset. I was upset. The coconut water was yucky. And it did not help the reputation of upside-down magic in our school community."

Marigold hung her head. "I'm sorry."

"I know. But it was much too early to try a new skill out on human subjects. Much, much too early." He leaned forward. "You're still learning, Marigold. You're both still learning. I understand how a mistake like this could happen, but it cannot happen again."

He cleared his throat. "You already know that students are not allowed to make other students invisible or levitate. That is a school rule. But as of today, I will be adopting a new policy to include shrinking. It will be called the No Alterations Policy. There will be no alterations of fellow students or teachers, including turning people invisible, levitating them, *or* shrinking them. All other magical alterations count as well. So if you find yourself able to grow wings on people, or turn their arms to stone, or anything like that, it is forbidden here at Dunwiddle, for the safety of all students and teachers. Do you understand? Hmm?"

Marigold and Nory nodded.

"Good," he said. "And although I do not want to punish students for a peaceful protest, I do think there should be consequences for having used your magic on humans in a way that sent them to the hospital. Do you agree?"

"Yes," squeaked Marigold.

"So I would like you to do some community service in the library," said the principal. "Mr. Wang has had some flaring issues in there recently, and he needs help with cleanup and with the general running of the library, sorting books and shelving and so forth. Marigold, you will go there during recess Monday through Thursday for the next three weeks, as a way of taking seriously the problems that your careless use of magic caused for this school."

"Okay," said Marigold. She was actually relieved to have something to do.

"Do I have to do anything?" asked Nory.

The principal nodded. "I signed you up for four days of helping Coach clean out the gym storage. Lots of old smelly uniforms and dirty balls of yarn in there. They could use organizing."

Nory sighed. "All right. Sounds fair."

Marigold hesitated. "And what about the Dreggs?" she asked. "Is there any way you would consider letting us bring them to school? I understand that they are disruptive, I really do, but they have also been really great for helping UDM kids feel included with the other kids."

She saw Nory's eyes widen.

Principal Gonzalez looked back and forth between them. "The Dreggs are extremely disruptive. But I do see your point. And I am willing to stand by the offer I made to you yesterday. Students can bring Dreggs to school every Friday, to be taken out only during recess. Never in the classroom, never in the cafeteria—only in the yard on Fridays."

"Really?" Nory squealed.

Marigold couldn't believe it.

"Yes. In fact, that's why I gave you Fridays off from your community-service recess jobs. However, all Dreggs should be kept in students' lockers and only hatched outside. Any Dreggs hatched inside a hallway or a classroom will be confiscated immediately and until the end of the year. Understood?"

They both nodded.

"Good. I'll make an announcement later today, and will send home an email. Now back to class, kids."

They hurried out of his office. Nory squeezed Marigold's hand. "Good job. I never would have asked him to stop the Dreggs ban after everything that happened. That was awesome."

Marigold smiled. She'd have Friday recesses with Sparkle-Puff and Tootsie! And the principal had met her one-fortieth of the way there. Now, that seemed pretty awesome.

21

On the first Friday of December, the weather was gloriously sunny and cold. Nory had a pocket full of Dreggs and a happy, fizzy energy inside her.

At recess, she climbed on top of the picnic table at the far end of the yard and held both hands up for attention. The kids gathered around her grew quiet. Those who were still mad about the whole shrinking fiasco—and there were plenty of them—narrowed their eyes and made growly faces from farther off. Oh, well. Too bad for them!

"Does everyone have their Dreggs out?" Nory asked.

"Not yet," said Bax. But he pulled one from his pocket.

"Yes," cried Elliott, Willa, Pepper, and Marigold. Marigold thrust hers into the sky.

"Welcome to *Dregg Dash Fridays*!" cried Nory. "Let the Dregg Dash begin!"

All the kids squeezed their Dreggs to launch the hatching process.

Nory hopped down among them as they set their Dreggs on the picnic table, and laughed at the surge of farting sounds. *Now this is the life*, she thought, admiring the newest Dregg in her collection, just as it cracked open. It was small and magenta—and it hatched into the cutest Blurper Dragon ever! Nory named it Roarie, after the real live Blurper she'd met at the dragon rescue center.

Clyde ran over with Rainey. "Guys!" he called. "Hey, guys! Guess what!"

"Clyde! Rainey!" Nory cried. "Where are your Dreggs?"

"We've got them, don't worry," Clyde said.

"But wait till you see what Clyde has," Rainey said. "It's even better than Dreggs."

"Better than Dreggs? Never," Nory scoffed, though she was curious. "What is it?"

Clyde beamed. "Watch!" He bent over at the waist and tugged first at his right shoelaces and then at his left. He stood up, looking pleased.

"Um, those are shoelaces," said Nory. "Not that fun, actually."

"Wait for it, wait for it," Clyde said. Then *whoosh!* Up he shot, pinwheeling his arms to maintain his balance and laughing hysterically. At first Nory thought he'd grown a foot taller, but on closer inspection, she saw that only his shoes had grown. They'd puffed up to ten times their size, and Clyde perched on top of them.

"Show them the rest! Go on," encouraged Rainey. "Ready, set . . . go!"

Clyde lifted one puffy shoe and took a step. Then another and another. He picked up speed, and *boing! Boing! Boing!*

He galumphed around the playground in huge bouncy bounds, soaring high into the air with each step before barreling back down. "They're called Moon Boppers," he yelled as he ran. "Because it's like walking on the moon. *Running* on the moon!"

Elliott chased after him. "I want to try," he said. "Can I try?"

"Only after I try," said Rainey, running to keep up with Elliott. "I get first dibs, don't I, Clyde?"

Everyone followed. They stuffed their Dreggs into their pockets and forgot all about them. Willa even left hers behind. Nory squatted and scooped it up, stroking its bitsy head. "Well, that stinks," Nory said.

"Clyde's Moon Boppers?" Marigold said. She had stayed behind. "I don't know. I think they're cool."

"Super cool," said Nory. "But still. People shouldn't forget about Dreggs just because something new comes along. We just got permission to bring them on Fridays!"

"Hmm," said Marigold. Her eyes followed Clyde as he bopped around the playground. "They do look fun," she said. "And . . . there's no rule against them, right? I mean, we could still have Dregg Dash Fridays. But we could also have Moon Bopper Mondays."

"Yes," Nory exclaimed. "Marigold, you're a genius!"

"I am, aren't I?" said Marigold.

"Come on," Nory said, grabbing her hand and pulling her across the playground toward Clyde. "We have *got* to put this plan into action!"

Acknowledgments

Massive, bigged-up thanks to the team at Scholastic, including but not limited to: David Levithan, Rachel Feld, Maya Marlette, Charisse Meloto, Taylan Salvati, Lisa Bourne, Sue Flynn, Melissa Schirmer, Emily Heddleson, Robin Hoffman, Lizette Serrano, Abby Denning, and Aimee Friedman. Colossal appreciation for Laura Dail, Tamar Rydzinski, Barry Goldblatt, Tricia Ready, Elizabeth Kaplan, Lauren Kisilevsky, Eddie Gamarra, Lauren Walters, Katie-Rose Summerfield, Alyssa Stonoha, and Deb Shapiro. Immense gratitude for Bob, for all the support.

We are, as always, humongously grateful to Randy, Daniel, and Todd, and our tinies, Al, Jamie, Maya, Mirabelle, Alisha, Ivy, Hazel, Chloe, and Anabelle. And finally, we thank all of our readers! We love each and every one of you, big or small.

Nory, Marigold, and friends return for another upside-down adventure in:

UPSIDE★DOWN MAGIC #7: HIDE AND SEEK

About the Authors

SARAH MLYNOWSKI is the author of many books for tweens, teens, and adults, including the *New York Times* bestselling Whatever After series, the Magic in Manhattan series, and *Gimme a Call*. She is also the co-creator of the traveling middle-grade book festival OMG BookFest. She would like to be a Flicker so she could make the mess in her room invisible. Visit her online at sarahm.com.

LAUREN MYRACLE is the *New York Times* best-selling author of many books for young readers, including the Winnie Years series, the Flower Power series, and the Life of Ty series. *The Backward Season* is the most recent book in her Wishing Day trilogy. She would like to be a Fuzzy so she could talk to unicorns and feed them berries. You can find Lauren online at laurenmyracle.com.

EMILY JENKINS is the author of many chapter books, including *Brave Red, Smart Frog*; the Toys Trilogy (which begins with *Toys Go Out*); and the Invisible Inkling series. Her picture books include *All-of-a-Kind Family Hanukkah*; *A Greyhound, A Groundhog*; *Princessland*; *Lemonade in Winter*; and *Toys Meet Snow*. She would like to be a Flare and work as a pastry chef. Visit Emily at emilyjenkins.com.